Redeeming

Book Three of the Kirin Lane Series

By Kelley Griffin

Print ISBN: 978-1-958965-04-7,
eBook ISBN: 978-1-958965-03-0
Hardcover ISBN: 978-1-958965-14-6

Cover Art by Amor Paloma Designs, LLC
Edited by

Produced in the United States of America

Griffin, Kelley
Redeeming, Book Three of the Kirin Lane Series

This is a work of fiction. The characters and events in this book are a product of the author's imagination and are used fictitiously. Any similarity to real people, living or dead, business establishments, events or locales is entirely coincidental.

March 2023

Dedication

To my sons.

You guys make me laugh, hug me tightly, are loyal and loving and you challenge me every day to be a better human just by your examples. I have no doubt that with all your God given talents, you will all achieve all your dreams.

I'm so proud of the five of you.

You are my biggest accomplishment.

Love you more,

~Mom

To my friend, Rhonda Ferguson.

Thank you for your time, talent, friendship, and willingness to always give me a yes when I need a trusted friend to read my manuscript first.

I'm so grateful to you!

~Kelley

Dear Reader,

Thank you for reading the final installment of the Kirin Lane story. WHOO HOO!!

Kirin wants to destroy this human trafficking ring, once and for all, but to do that, she'll have to work with her worst enemy and come to terms with her own shortcomings. Will she be able to keep her family together or will her past mistakes cost her the one man who is supposed to love her the most?

I'd love to hear from you. Please consider taking a minute to leave a review. It's one of the best compliments.

XO~
Kelley

Facebook: Kelley Griffin Author
Goodreads: Kelley Griffin Author
BookBub: Kelley-Griffin
Twitter: @AuthorKTGriffin
Instagram: Kelleygriffinauthor

<u>Other titles by Kelley Griffin</u>

Binding Circumstance

The Kirin Lane Series:
Entangling, Book One of the Kirin Lane Series
Unraveling, Book Two of the Kirin Lane Series
Redeeming, Book Three of the Kirin Lane Series

The Casey King Series:
A Mind Unequal, Book One of the Casey King Series

Taken for Granted

Two Weeks Before...

3am.

A young girl, dressed all in black, crouched in the dark behind a rank-smelling green dumpster. That same dumpster was the only thing that separated her from the overgrown field behind the strip mall. It was the only reason they couldn't see her.

She glanced side to side. The quiet of the back alley only made her heartbeat seem louder. She rubbed her face as a war waged on internally. Then, out of habit, pulled her dark hair back and pulled it in a high pony using the hair tie she always kept on her wrist.

Just like her, they watched the back door. She was sure of it. Her plan had to work. Her family had been through so much already. But she was determined to find her sister. But in order to do that, she'd have to go back in.

Shaking her head, she let out the breath she'd been holding. Her younger sister's sweet but sarcastic voice echoed in her mind telling her she was a certifiable nut-bag for doing this.

God, how much she wanted to hear that annoying voice again. Anger flashed through her as she gritted her teeth. Yes. She *would* see her sister again, even if it killed her.

Neither of them had asked for this. They were good kids—well, in truth, her sister was.

She, however, was more opinionated and vocal than most her age. Then again, most girls her age were more worried about clothes and boys and going to stupid places like the mall.

Here she was, hiding behind a dumpster with nothing except a tiny backpack filled with the one memento she'd never let them have, trying to take down a trafficking ring and steal her sister back.

They'd been orphans in the foster system. Their real parents were either in jail or dead. Didn't know and didn't care. If she'd been a few years older, she could've raised her sister by herself. But as it was, she wasn't even old enough to drive, let alone raise another human. If she ever found out that her jack-tard foster father, who hated them both, had anything to do with their abductions, she'd find his broke ass and kill him.

Just then, the tall grass illuminated only by moonlight on the other side of the alley jerked as two dark shadows moved into position. Yep, they were here. A shudder ran down her spine.

This was the third night spotters had tagged the attractive female liquor store worker's vehicle by placing a black zip tie on the back passenger side door handle. Third night. In the underworld, even she knew that meant the occupant would be taken.

She checked her watch. 3:10. She'd already scoped out the front of the store earlier as she'd walked past to grab some gum from the convenience store next to the strip mall and saw that the woman's co-worker had left early, looking pale.

She'd wondered if they'd paid him to go so, the woman would be an easier target. They used any available tactic they could to get a girl alone.

One thing she always prided herself on was her ability to watch people. To pick out the smallest details. Their weaknesses and strengths. It was a gift that didn't always serve her well.

The back door squeaked, and she froze. It opened briefly then shut again as if the young woman had forgotten something. Suddenly, the back light flicked on and exposed the girl's hiding place.

She sucked in a quick breath, but then stayed completely still. If she was lucky, the abductors on the other side of the alley in the weeds would think she was just a box or a garbage bag.

The young woman peeked her head out. She looked to be in her twenties, blonde hair and slim built. She held something in her hand, mace maybe. *Crap.* If that scared these scabs off and they didn't take her, the girl would lose another precious day trying to save her sister.

She had to do something.

Just as she was about to stand and make a noise, the girl yelled in the darkness.

2

"I saw you, *homeless girl.* I know you're out here. And if you're here to rob me, all the money is in a locked safe with a timer on it that I can't open. I personally only have three dollars," her voice trembled as she added, "and I'll give it to you if you show yourself."

Even though her voice shook, it was also surprisingly firm.

Quickly, the girl took her hair down and messed it up a little to get into character. She strolled slowly out of the shadow of the dumpster with her hands up, trying not to look toward the shadows across the alley.

"I'm not trying to rob you," the dark headed girl said quietly as the young woman spun and with a shaky hand, aimed her weapon toward the girl. The young woman narrowed her gaze.

"Oh, really? So, you're just out here for a stroll?"

Hands still up as in surrender and walking toward her like someone trying not to spook a deer, the younger girl smiled reassuringly and whispered, "Your car was tagged, which means they're going to abduct you tonight."

The woman's arm lowered slightly as her gaze darted out at the tall grass next to where she'd parked her car.

"What do I do?"

"I don't know," she said, "but I know we can't outrun them."

The young woman stared at the girl like she was seeing her for the first time. "So, you're *in* with them? Are you the bait?" She sounded angry now.

The dark headed girl shook her head no, then added, "It happened to me before. I escaped, but then I saw they tagged you. I was trying to warn you."

Just then, identical to the first time, she heard a twig snap behind her. She turned in time to see the cloth coming at her mouth and nose. Even though she knew it was coming, she still screamed.

And then nothing.

~*~

One week before…

It all started with a tomato.

Kirin Lane stepped out into her dimly lit garage smiling to herself and precariously holding two objects. With some difficulty, she softly shut the door behind her. It was even too early for the sun to be up.

With her record of being clumsy, sneaking up on someone with full hands was a bigger feat than she gave herself credit for.

Sam Neal hummed, earbuds in as usual, as he laid under her car on a rolling creeper to change her oil.

Kirin snuck around the SUV and stopped, staring at two muscular legs in work jeans sticking out from under the car.

"Lane," he said, letting her know she didn't catch him off-guard.

Kirin grinned to herself and said nothing. She tapped her foot against his shoe.

"Look," Sam said, still under the car, "I know you said not to make plans today, which is why I got up *early* so I could change your oil."

Kirin bit her lip and tapped his shoe again.

Her favorite two strong hands grabbed the underside of her truck and rolled the scooter out.

Sam smiled as if he'd been caught with his hand in the cookie jar. When their eyes met, Kirin smiled at him with both hands behind her back. Finally, she finally spoke.

"Right hand or left?"

"Depends," he sat up, tucked his earbuds into his pocket and answered with a crooked smile.

"On?"

"Which one will I want more?"

The twinkle in his eye told her they were no longer talking about the items behind her back.

"Oh, I think you'll want it all."

Sam smiled. That full-on, amused, sexy smile that even after all this time, made her get weak in the knees. He stood and took a step toward her, close enough she could feel his warm breath in her hair. Soft hands settled in around her waist. He never took his eyes off her.

"Well, as usual Ms. Lane, you're right about that." Sam kissed her forehead and spread out his stance, so their eyes were level.

"I smell coffee," he whispered.

"Right or left?" she asked again, quietly.

He tried to sneak a look around her. She raised her chin and shook her head.

Sam exhaled playfully, "Left."

Kirin slowly brought her left hand around her body.

Sam reached out and picked the object from her hand, eyebrows furrowed and staring at it like she'd just handed him a rat.

"You want me to eat a tomato for breakfast?" His voice was higher pitched than normal.

Kirin shook her head and laughed, "Today is the anniversary of the day I met you down at Morrissey's grocery store. I thought a reminder of that day would be fitting."

Sam chuckled, "God, you were so cute that day."

"*Cute?*" Kirin asked, her face scrunched up.

Sam's demeanor changed from jovial to dead serious.

"I'm sorry. Misspoke. Can I say, *sexy as hell,* to the woman I'm marrying in three weeks?"

Kirin smiled, "You can."

Sam nuzzled in closer, then remembered the coffee. Taking it from her hand, he took a quick sip, smiled gratefully, then placed it on top of her truck.

"We have time, right?" Sam whispered, burrowing back in, and kissing her neck briefly. He pulled back and touched his nose to hers. His eyes closed.

"We always have time," she whispered back.

The day before…

Sam Neal blew out the breath he was holding. He knew he was in the wrong. He adjusted the small pack at his feet and resituated the airplane seat belt so he could scoot closer to the aisle and away from the loud businessman crammed into the seat next to him.

He'd made Kirin a promise. He'd sworn to his soon-to-be wife—no more missions. Especially since they only had two weeks until their wedding.

But this time, it was unavoidable.

The intel he'd been fed told him *she* was the target.

Better to stop them in their tracks than let them get close to her. Nope. He'd come too far to lose her now.

So, he'd break the promise. Big deal. She'd be off the hit list, and he'd be back with tons of time to spare for the wedding.

He'd get off the plane, rescue a girl, kill the man who put a hit out on the woman he loved and fly home.

Easy.

Until it wasn't.

Chapter One
Friday

Damnit.

Kirin Lane pressed the pedal to the floor. An East Tennessee pounding Spring rain mixed with her erratic driving meant that her SUV tires slid then barked as they grabbed the pavement. Groaning, the vehicle jerked like someone waking from a nightmare. Cars bogged up the far-right exit ramp like they were waiting in line for the newest ride at Dollywood.

Kirin darted toward a small opening between a semi-truck and a black car as if she were playing a dangerous game of Frogger.

Yes, she was driving like a lunatic. But she had good reason. Her fear and guilt over what she'd done, were racing to see which could make her the craziest.

She'd always been a horrible liar. Like the worst. And yet, she'd kept a secret from the man she loved more than anything for two months. Two long months.

Her phone buzzed for the second time.

Kirin shook that familiar problem out of her head. Right now, she needed answers.

Sam hadn't answered her texts all day. She tried telling herself that maybe he'd left his phone somewhere. Or he was just busy.

But the text she'd received from a blocked number confirmed her fears.

Exhaling, she tried to slow her heart rate.

Maybe, he'd found out her secret. He'd discovered she'd been lying to him. Maybe he decided he didn't want to marry her now that she was damaged.

It all started a few months back. Sam, Steve and two of their FBI buddies embarked on a weeklong caribou hunting trip in Alaska.

Sam's idea of a bachelor party.

She'd driven them to the airport, all boisterous and laughing. Once she parked outside the terminal doors, they'd all dove out of her SUV like they were on a mission. She'd stood at the back of her SUV handing each one their bag. One by one they thanked her, hugged her, and strutted toward the large glass airport doors.

But not Sam.

As soon as she'd turned back to grab his bag and pull it toward the open hatch of her SUV, Sam had pinned her. He'd stepped close and wrapped muscular arms around her. Kirin leaned backward, into him, getting one last deep breath of the scent that was pure Sam.

Gently he turned her around and in one quick movement, he grabbed her waist, scooped her up off the ground and lifted her to sit. It was the same giddy feeling she'd had the first day they'd met, when he'd lifted her onto his tailgate, the day she'd been attacked outside the grocery store.

Leaning over and with his arms propping his body up on either side of her, his face was nose to nose with hers. She'd laughed a little until she realized the serious look on his face. He had something to say.

She'd smiled at him, big. He returned it. That green-eyed stare that told her she was his everything. That same stare that always melted her into a puddle. Then finally he spoke.

"Lane. This is the first time in three years I won't be watching over you."

Kirin nodded. Out of habit, she rubbed the muscles along his strong arms, as that amazing Sam smell invaded her entire being.

"Promise me something?"

"Sure."

"No hero stuff. Stay put and don't go anywhere alone." She had nodded. "Keep your location *on*, okay?"

Kirin lifted one hand and put it to his cheek. "We'll be fine. Go have fun, okay?"

Sam nodded.

"Love you."

Sam always said it first.

"Love you, more."

She'd always answered.

Gently Sam lowered her to the ground, gave her one more squeeze, then grabbed his bags just as his buddies started hollering at him from the door to hurry up.

Sam rolled his eyes at them, took one more last look at her, mouthed, *love you*, one last time and then disappeared behind the sliding glass doors.

Kirin climbed back in and began her thirty-five-minute drive home.

But.

The weirdest thing happened.

Headed down Alcoa Highway toward home, Kirin felt a sharp pain in her side that made her swerve and took her breath away. She almost pulled over. But then it was gone as quickly as it came on.

Blowing it off, she drove the rest of the way home and went about her Sunday cleaning, taking care of the boys, and tying up some loose ends for their upcoming wedding.

But by early Monday morning, she was in excruciating pain. So much so, that even now, her memories were spotty at best. She barely remembered driving herself to the ER after dropping the boys off at school that morning.

Or the sweet video Steve had sent of the guy's first night in Alaska where Sam had been bought one too many drinks at the local pub in the village. On camera, he'd hugged and told every man at the bar how they all needed someone honest, loyal, and loving, like his Kirin.

God she was a dishonest dirtbag.

She didn't even remember talking to Rosa that morning, or her aunt and uncle, but she knew she had. She was sure she sounded like a meth addict in that conversation.

She'd made them all promise not to tell the boys or Sam.

Tuesday morning, she woke in a white hospital room to find a bald doctor in scrubs staring at her, expectantly.

"Hello. I was your surgeon, Dr. Stallings." He sounded part bored and part robot, as if he'd practiced the speech several times.

Very matter-of-factly he announced that he'd performed an emergency laparoscopic Unilateral Salpingectomy overnight.

Kirin stared at him and when she found her voice, it was hoarse. "Sorry. I don't know what that is."

"We removed one wretched, infected fallopian tube and strongly considered the removal of the other one as well."

Her heart dropped into her stomach. "Wait...you didn't though, right?"

The man narrowed clear blue eyes at her before answering, "No, but I should have. Thanks to a heavy endometriosis network, that second tube is kinked over onto itself and the chances of it working correctly are very slim. I'd say you've got a 2% chance of getting pregnant now, but at your age, it's probably less. We're sending the other fallopian tube off to the lab to ensure it's benign. You should receive results in a week or so."

When he'd finished speaking, he promptly stood, nodded, and walked out, pulling the door closed behind him.

Kirin had sat in the silence and stared at the blank wall as his words hung in the air.

2%.

Like she didn't have enough stacked against her. And yes, being slightly over forty wasn't exactly one foot in the grave, but it sure made docs label her as "high risk for pregnancy" faster than you could say *perimenopause.*

As the weight of his words hit her, it was all Kirin could do to keep it together, until she couldn't.

Sam.

All he'd ever wanted was a family.

Oh, he loved her boys, that was apparent on the daily, but she knew he longed for a child that was his.

And now, there was a 98% chance she couldn't give it to him.

Kirin's mind jumbled and twisted as she drove remembering that same sorrow and grief that had gripped her that morning. Her hand immediately touched the tiny half inch cut on her belly.

There're reasons people shouldn't drive distracted.

No sooner had she clicked off her blinker after sliding in front of the semi, than the sleek black car directly in front of her took a nosedive.

Standing on her brake pedal she cursed and willed her 4Runner not to hit it. Kirin screamed as the contents of her entire car slid toward the front like a giant had picked up her vehicle and shook it. Her tires howled in complaint. Thank God the semi had enough sense to keep its distance and not hit her.

"Idiot," she mumbled to herself, picking up the contents of her purse from the passenger side floorboard.

When traffic resumed, she let out the breath she didn't know she had held.

After the surgery, when Sam and the others had returned from their trip a week later with stories of campfire antics, large caribou that got away, and her big tough spy talking about their wedding like a twenty-something woman, Kirin had healed physically, gotten back to work and shoved the sadness down deep.

The weeks that followed, she wrestled with the idea of telling him. What if he decided his desire to have kids was bigger than his love for her?

It didn't matter. He deserved to know the truth. She knew that.

So, she decided she would not marry him unless he knew the truth. That was fair.

And she'd tried to tell him.

She really had.

But every time she'd pluck up the courage to let him know what had happened, one of the boys would walk in or she wouldn't want to spoil the nice family evening they were having.

In truth, they'd both been so busy rushing around getting things done for the wedding, some evenings they barely saw each other. There was just never a right time.

God, she was such a horrible human for not telling him yet.

The boys had been told she'd spent a couple of days with her friend Stacy, trying to help her through her PTSD from being tortured at the hands of the leader of the mob, after Sal died, Nicky and her misguided, late fiancé, Todd.

Part of her couldn't bear the sadness she'd see in those strong green eyes, but she was determined. He deserved to know.

It had eaten at her subconscious. She'd withheld the whole experience and information from the one man she needed the most when sad things happened. The man she was two weeks away from marrying.

Every day since had been like watching the numbers countdown on a timer attached to a bomb and knowing that she only had a few more days to come clean.

Would Sam still want to marry her? She wasn't sure, but she prayed he'd find it in his soul to forgive her for not telling him.

But, right now, even if she had the courage to confess, she couldn't.

Because Sam Neal, the love of her life, was missing.

Maybe he'd found out the secret and bolted. Or someone from the hospital had called to check on her after the procedure and gotten him instead. No, they had strict instructions to only call her cell. Then again, they were human.

Or…maybe Laura had been right.

Her friend's words had haunted Kirin since Christmas.

"Sam's not who you think he is!"

And now, Laura was fighting a brain injury to regain mobility and independence, all while slowly uncovering the details of her former underground life.

While her other best friend, Stacy, struggled with being completely happy with her new beau Brandon one minute and fighting PTSD episodes the next.

Sam had become increasingly aloof and stressed as he juggled both his regular job and his after-hours hobby. Working with Stacy's brother Steve and the FBI to take down any remaining operatives in The Club was a passion, but tough on him just the same.

Plus, he'd been hiding something.

Kirin could always tell. She'd tried to get it out of him a few times, but nothing worked. He was locked up tight on that one.

She couldn't fault him for lying to her. Not now, especially since she'd been keeping something from him as well. And that stuck in her craw like swallowing a large bite of a hardboiled egg.

Sam had given her his word. No more missions and no more heroics. He'd sworn nothing could stop them from finally walking down the aisle, or in their case, their backyard next to the woods, in two weeks.

Two weeks.

But she feared his promises had been empty.

And now...he'd ghosted.

Her windshield wipers slapped angrily. But even the rain was no match for the storm brewing inside Kirin's mind. She cracked her window for some fresh air.

Spring hadn't fully emerged from the deadness of winter, but it was trying as the temps rose above sixty in the afternoon, but at night it would dip back down to the thirties. Bright green leaves cradled little pink flowers everywhere and the air smelled of rain and Dogwoods.

But something else loomed too. It was as if Spring were trying to signal that their troubles were over.

Only Kirin knew better.

She bit her pinky nail as she drove. At the redlight at the end of the offramp, she reread the text.

Your fiancé is no longer your concern.

~*~

Kirin paced the worn spot in her wooden floor as supper cooked on the stove. The boys loved her goulash, but today the smell turned her stomach. Maybe it was just nerves.

Will and Jack, her ever-growing boys, had asked when Sam would be home. She was through lying.

Kirin, facing the stove, told them she hadn't heard from him today, and left it at that. She turned in time to see Will's eyebrows furrow as if he was trying to guess why.

When she shot him a comforting smile, he nodded then raced Jack up the steps to play video games until dinnertime.

Kirin was grateful there was no inquisition and for the time to think, but she knew, when Jack took a bath, there would be questions.

Rosa had hugged her tight before she left for the day, mumbling about some errand she'd been dreading. So, it was just Kirin, the rain pelting down, and her imagination running wild.

A text from Steve confirmed her fears.

Sam home?

Kirin snatched her phone next to the goulash spoon and answered,

No. Do you know where he is?

Eyes wide and standing stock still, Kirin watched her phone like a bomb. Three dots indicated that Steve was replying, but nothing came through.

After dinner dishes were loaded and the boys were doing homework, Kirin checked again for a response.

When it rang in her hand, she jumped. The caller-id name at the top read, *Evil Woman.*

Great. The only woman she'd ever truly hated. The one who'd tried unsuccessfully to take her Sam away. She'd better not have had anything to do with Sam's disappearance.

Kirin gritted her teeth and answered. "What do you want?"

"Making dinner?" Gianna's tone made it sound like Kirin was gutting a beaver, although clearly, she was attempting to sound pleasant.

"As usual."

"Don't you ever go out?" Gianna asked sincerely.

Kirin pinched the bridge of her nose and answered as plainly as she could, "Saving for a wedding. Did you need something?"

Gianna cleared her throat.

Kirin knew, at the mention of the word wedding, Gianna always clammed up. She couldn't tell if it was because the pretentious woman secretly wanted one of her own with a certain FBI agent but would never stoop so low as to say it, or if she was just jealous that Kirin and Sam had something she didn't.

"I know we made an agreement not to do this, but it's urgent that I speak to Sam and he's not answering. Have you heard from him today?"

Tiny hairs stood on the back of her neck. Gianna was supposedly now working on the side of good.

For today.

But the thought of the two of them talking still sent her mind into a jealous tailspin. And the last dang thing that Kirin wanted was to admit to this woman that she didn't know where her soon-to-be husband was, so she did what any red-blooded woman would do with a woman who had previously *wanted* her man…she bent the truth.

"He's been busy. Want me to have him call you when he's free?"

Gianna hesitated.

Either she didn't believe Kirin's story, or she knew more than she was saying. "Never mind Lane, I'll find him myself." And with that, she hung up.

Kirin immediately texted Steve.

Seriously. Where is he?

Three dots indicated he was finally writing back.

Gone. Off grid. The tracking has been turned off. What time do the boys go down?

Kirin stared at her phone.

It took her a full minute to gather herself. Sam had been acting erratically, but Sam was the one who'd warned *her* over and over, never to turn off tracking. It was the only way they could find each other.

Yet, for some reason, he had.

"Nine," she texted.

See you then.

Chapter Two

Steve knew this wouldn't work.

He let out a long breath as he slammed his truck into gear in front of her house.

He'd grappled for years trying to do the right thing. To prove himself, first in the TBI and finally in the FBI. Clearly, he was on the side of good.

But lately, where the lines between good and evil had always been clear as a crisp fall day, those lines, especially when they involved one tall, beautiful, strong-willed, complicated as they come, woman…were now blurred.

She'd slowly become the person that he needed to text first thing in the morning and the last person he did before bed, even if they were fighting, or *bantering* as she liked to call it, which was pretty much 24/7.

The only other thing in his life he'd spent more time on was his career in the FBI.

Steve rubbed his face as his mind drifted back. He'd done something unsanctioned and dishonest. It ate at him night and day, but he just couldn't help it. He had to protect her stubborn ass no matter what. And if he lost his career or she never forgave him…well, that would be the ultimate cost, but he'd set that ball in motion all over again if he had to.

Quickly, he whipped out his phone, punched in numbers, slammed his eyes shut and listened for an answer.

"Operation Redeeming is a go," he said through gritted teeth.

The line clicked.

He stowed his phone and hoped like hell it would be successful. So many moving parts to this one. He just prayed he could get them all back alive.

Interrupting his thoughts, a petite, brown-haired young girl with a guarded smile stepped out of the front door and onto the stoop in the light mist of the rain. When she caught sight of his truck, she grinned shyly and waved at him. From the inside of his truck, he waved back with a ridiculously wide grin. That little one had him wrapped around her tiny finger almost as much as her new mama did.

Paloma stepped back inside and stood next to a white-haired woman with dark skin and a kind face like someone's grandma. The new sign had been placed on the giant, antique wooden front door proclaiming the old house as the newly founded *Eugenia Williams Foundation for Girls.*

Gianna stepped between them and then out onto the stoop, opened her umbrella and bent to kiss the girl on the cheek. When she raised back up, the girl lifted both hands and crossed her fingers. Gianna nodded, then patted the arm of the older woman and watched until the large wooden door closed.

When she turned, she gave a quick glare toward Steve's truck. She pushed her shoulders back and chin high and walked briskly in the rain to Steve's truck.

When he opened his door to walk around and open hers, she waved him off. He didn't care. He shook his head, trotted around the back and opened her door anyway.

Gianna's silky long hair was twisted up in a pretty bun with dark, shiny pieces that curled down the back of her neck. She wore a tailored top in soft pink that lightly hugged every curve along with designer jeans that probably cost more than his last paycheck. Dark pumps hugged her pretty feet. Her outfit along with the sweet-smelling perfume that dang dropped his defenses down two notches, suggested this was a date.

It wasn't. He knew better.

"Stop," she said, pinning him with those gorgeous eyes as soon as they each closed their doors.

"What?" he said, hands up in surrender and half laughing. "I haven't said a word."

"You're giving me the look."

Steve grinned and turned his body toward hers.

"What look?"

"You know exactly what look," she replied quick as she pulled the seatbelt across her body and clicked it.

Steve's eyebrows rose, but he didn't look away, waiting for an explanation.

Gianna exhaled, "The look that says you've seen me naked."

Steve grinned. He loved it when she squirmed.

"I love that look."

Gianna turned her body toward his, "It was one time and we both agreed it was a mistake."

"Negative. I did not agree with that. And if memory serves, it was twice."

"Well," she stammered, looking out the windshield, "I..." she paused, turned her gaze toward him again and pointed a finger, "it's not going to happen again, understood?"

Steve stared at her for a moment longer. She froze, and just as her gaze raked him up and down and landed on his chest, he detected a slight lean toward him. The air crackled. When she suddenly broke eye contact and scooted away, he shook his head and put the truck in reverse, but didn't push the gas.

"Whatever you say, boss."

When she stared out the window, he decided the night was already headed downhill, why not poke the bear, and see if he could get any more information out of her.

"So, you gonna tell me what you found?"

She slid him a look that said, *Hell no*. "We've been over this. I don't have anything you need to know about. I'm going to finish the job that *your team* didn't do. I gave you intel last time and you didn't produce, so I'm going on my own to get the girl."

Steve gritted his teeth. The mission itself had been a success, they'd saved fourteen girls and put eight of the bad guys' nastiest runners in jail, but the boss had taken one girl out just before they arrived. The one Gianna wanted.

Arianna.

It was as if they'd been tipped off early, exactly who his agents were looking for. As he turned the first of several corners to get to Kirin's house he asked, "So you're telling me, you're gonna waltz right in there, with no bargaining chip, and you think they're just gonna hand her over and then let you go?"

Gianna exhaled loudly, "No. I'm going to reason with—"

"Counsel..." his booming voice interrupted her and he slammed the truck back into park. "Please tell me you're not going in there with a "puppies and kitties"" attitude that you're gonna change them and they'll just smile and let you go."

At this, the bear was poked.

Gianna turned her body toward him, and he could've sworn that fire came out of her eyes.

"Of course, I'm not! I always have a plan B, I'm just not telling you because your guys will screw it up. I'm not naïve! And stop calling me Counsel!" She said this last bit through gritted teeth.

Gianna went from shaking her fists at him to crossing her arms and glaring out the side window. God he was crazy about this woman. But she was going to get taken, and damnit he was not about to let that happen.

Softening his voice, he called to her.

"G."

When she didn't turn, he took her hand and pleaded, "G, look at me."

She turned, looking red-faced and a bit disheveled. She glared at him like she'd enjoy every second of stabbing him in the throat with a pen. But curiously, she didn't seem to mind his hand holding hers. When she finally locked eyes with him, he spoke. "I don't want to lose you. I know you're capable, strong, smart and God knows crafty..."

At this her lips tugged up slightly and she glanced down.

"But those people are gonna take one look at you, and they're going to want to keep you." Steve paused waited for her gaze to meet his. He shook his head, "And that doesn't work for me."

He stared into her eyes. Hers were softening and thoughtful as if his words had melted a small part of that tough outer shell. Then, like a light switch, she turned, dropped his hand, and stared back out the window.

"We both know why this," she gestured to the space between them, "doesn't work."

"I don't think we do," Steve said quietly.

Gianna whispered, "It's the lion falling for the lamb."

Steve's back straightened, "Hold up, am I the lamb in this?" His voice was an octave or so higher than it should've been and he cleared his throat.

Gianna smiled and shook her head, "No, wait, not a good analogy. It's just…you're on the good side—the law abiding side, and well…historically, I've never been. I'm not good for you."

"But—" Gianna interrupted him, placing a finger over his lips.

"That's not what we're talking about today." Gianna lowered her voice to a whisper, "I *need* to do this. And not for me. I have to save one more. *Just one.* Then I'll get out."

When she lowered her finger from his lips, he watched her. She'd finally given the reason. His mind spun. She believed she was ruining him because of her past. Shit. How could he convince her that she was the reason he wanted to annihilate the mob? She was the reason he strove to be the best, so he could deserve her. She'd consumed his heart and mind a long time ago, and he wasn't going to let them take her. No matter what.

He might just be the only person on the planet that could tell when Gianna was being honest and real, but as she searched his eyes, he understood that right now, she was as vulnerable as she'd ever be. The fact that she could let her defensive brick wall down only with him made him feel like he was a superhero who could do anything. Steve clicked his seatbelt, put the truck in reverse and turned the truck around, then pushed the gas up the long and winding driveway toward the gate. When he stopped at the top to turn onto the main highway, he turned and spoke, "Promise me something."

"What?"

"Don't give up on this," Steve gestured to the space between them, just as she had, "until we've given it a proper chance, okay?"

Gianna watched him for a beat, then nodded. They drove in silence for the next several miles.

As they closed in, just a few roads away from Kirin's house, Gianna shifted nervously in her seat.

"Subject change?"

"Please," she exhaled. "Now, where is he?"

"You know damn good and well where he is."

"Does Kirin know?"

"She's about to. You're gonna tell her."

"She's gonna think I did this on purpose."

"Wouldn't you?"

She thought for a beat, then said, "Yes."

"Convince her otherwise."

Gianna visibly shuddered and for once, her tough exterior seemed to lower its shields.

Even though he knew she was withholding information and she'd gone behind his back, putting his best friend in harm's way, somewhere deep down, he still felt sorry for her.

As confident and strong willed as Gianna normally was, he knew he'd have to play referee to keep Kirin from killing her.

Chapter Three

Rosa stared at her niece, Rosita, or RD as her FBI team called her. Well, when they weren't calling her *Rookie*.

Her usual pixie-short, dark hair had been transformed. She now had long pretty locks, tight jeans that hugged her perfectly round booty, and a low-cut black top. The only thing that outwardly made her look like herself were her black sneakers. Her natural no-nonsense, pretty face was coated in more makeup than it had ever seen. If Rosa hadn't already known it was her, she would've never guessed.

"You look ridiculous," Rosa stated, matter-of-factly, as she subtly watched the throngs of people walking past. The two women shared a tight bond. If you asked Rosa, RD was lucky to have inherited Rosa's snarky sense of humor, especially in the face of a heavy situation.

"Thanks Tia. You make this job so much easier with your *encouraging* words."

RD slid her aunt a look, then resumed her scan of the crowded plaza inside Knoxville's newest and hippest downtown eateries, Marble City Market.

Businesswomen dressed in upscale casual attire with expensive handbags accompanied young men with trimmed beards dressed in skinny suits.

One side of the bottom floor of the massive building looked like a food court of elegant and eclectic eateries. Each establishment had its own counter and claim to fame. Every type of food from hand tossed authentic pizza to Italian penne to donuts and Greek gyros to a fully stocked martini bar. This posh place, set in the middle of what used to be an undesirable neighborhood, even had virtual Top Golf suites within its walls.

The sun was beginning to set and according to her niece, Saturday nights were always packed. RD's contact was somewhere inside.

Rosa knew the drill. She'd been privy to just enough information, but not all, for her protection. She knew that the only reason her niece had asked for her help was because this mission wasn't sanctioned. She couldn't rely on her FBI team to come and pull her out.

And that scared Rosa.

Her niece was tough, inside, and out. Jaded by a career where she had to prove that she was just as smart, determined, and hard wired as the other FBI men. *Jaded.* That was a great descriptor for her. Never time for a boyfriend or a life, everything revolved around getting ahead in the FBI. She was tenacious about this fact, having only slipped up once and told her aunt about a guy she liked, but in the end, she must've dropped him like a bad habit because of her work.

RD had made it clear exactly what she expected on this mission, but Rosa knew this girl had always had something up her sleeve and this dangerous excursion was based on a few spots of intel, a hunch, and an unofficial green light.

They were expecting an older heavy-set man of Asian descent, somewhere in his fifties, with piercing eyes. These were the only descriptors RD had been given. Rosa found herself watching the eyes of each man who walked by, so it took her completely by shock when an obese woman, dark skinned with a frown that said not to mess with her, walked up, grabbed RD roughly by the arm and dragged her toward the elevators, cursing her in Spanish.

This was not the cue they'd been told to look for, but after one backward glance from RD, Rosa immediately got into character.

Rosa mustered up her thickest accent, grabbed the large woman by the shirt and yanked her backward, until they were nose to nose. Rosa raised a fist and spoke directly into this woman's face in Spanish, *"Take your hands off my property! This one belongs to me."*

RD, head down and looking submissive, stepped on the woman's toes. The woman's gaze snapped from Rosa's angry face to RD's. Showing loyalty to your broker was a twisted sign of anyone being held captive, but Rosa knew it was part of her act.

The woman glared back at Rosa, got inches from her face and said through gritted teeth in perfect English, "I'm escorting you to the buyer. Stop making a scene. Is this your first time?"

Rosa thought for a beat, "At this market, yes."

The woman regained her hold on RD, pushed through the crowd to the elevators and the three walked on. When the doors shut, RD changed positions so that she stood next to Rosa. The woman didn't even seem to notice. She stared at the numbers as the elevator climbed.

When the numbers hit five, she turned.

"Does she speak English?"

Rosa answered, chin high, "Yes. She understands both languages, which is why she's so expensive."

The large woman waived her off as if she didn't care. Then spoke quickly in English.

"Listen. When this door opens, you'll turn right and walk her down to studio five on your left, it's a double unit with two simulator bays and no cameras. Knock three times and sit on the orange couch. Do not under any circumstances stare at the man's limp. And don't speak until spoken to."

When the doors opened on the top floor, Rosa grabbed RD by the arm and slowly walked to the right. RD pretended to scratch her nose but pointed toward the cameras at the end of the hall signaling to her aunt not to break character.

Rosa squeezed her niece's arm, which on the outside looked more like forcing the woman down the hall.

Though, in truth it was the squeeze of a woman terrified.

When they stopped in front of a large door with a "5" on it, Rosa hesitated. Was she really going to hand over her precious niece to these people? She'd been in the room with her sister when this creature was born.

Why on God's earth had she agreed to this awful plan?

RD must've felt her hesitation.

She mouthed I love you in Spanish, "*Te amo, Tia.*"

And knocked three times.

Chapter Four

Kirin had washed every dish, every stitch of clothing and was dusting for the second time that evening when Steve's truck pulled in the driveway.

She was grateful for any information, but she also felt like one of those military wives, when the officials came knocking at the door to break the news that a soldier had died in battle.

The pit of her stomach churned and then she heard a second door shut. Kirin sprinted to her front door and flung it open with a huge smile on her face. She knew Steve would find him.

That smile turned into a sneer as in the yellow dim light of her front porch, she watched a high heel hit the ground from the passenger side.

Damn.

What was *El Diablo* doing there?

Steve walked around the front of the vehicle and much to Kirin's surprise, rather than get the door for Gianna in his polite and casual way, he made a beeline for Kirin. Gianna's eyebrows furrowed and her mouth twitched.

She'd noticed it too.

As much as she still held a huge grudge toward Gianna, Kirin knew that Steve was head over heels, even if the brainiac hadn't figured it out himself. And by the look on Gianna's face, maybe she felt the same about him.

Steve took the farmhouse steps two at a time and embraced Kirin tightly.

"No news?" she asked quickly.

Steve pulled back from the embrace and shook his head.

Kirin turned and held the door for both her visitors although she thought briefly about tripping the second one. Steve went straight to the fridge and pulled out one of Sam's beers. As Gianna strutted through Kirin's front door, her face looked different. Nervous and less confident than she'd ever seen her. And what was worse was that she said nothing.

Holy crap.

No snarky comment about Kirin's wild hair or her "country" house or even the fact that she had on no makeup. No ribbing about being a homely housewife or, her favorite, *"Wow, who knew scrubs could be so sexy?"* comments.

This was a bad sign.

Kirin strolled around the corner and into the kitchen just as some unspoken thing was happening between Gianna and Steve.

His body was mainly inside Kirin's fridge, holding his beer bottle in one hand and raising a bottle of red with the other. His eyebrows rose playfully as if this was an inside joke. Gianna shot him a look that clearly said she didn't think it was funny. Steve shrugged, closed the fridge, and twisted the top off the beer, taking a long pull.

Gianna gingerly pulled out a chair so that it wouldn't drag across the wood floor and wake the boys.

When Kirin sat across from her, Steve suddenly struggled with where to sit, finally taking Sam's chair at the head of the table. It felt like a boardroom meeting where someone was about to die.

Gianna took a deep breath, held both hands up as if surrendering and began, "Sam is on a mission for me."

Flames shot through Kirin's eyes toward the evil woman. She must've been sabotaging the fact that Sam and Kirin were two weeks away from getting married. Kirin bit her lip as Steve worked to pry one of Will's pencils out of Kirin's grip. Kirin didn't even know she'd grabbed it and held it poised to stab Gianna when the moment arose.

Kirin glared but nodded for her to go on.

Gianna glanced nervously at Steve, then back at Kirin. Then she dug in her designer handbag and pulled out a picture. She slid it across the table to Kirin.

"My daughter, Paloma."

Kirin watched Gianna closely for a beat, then glanced down at the picture. The little girl had shiny dark hair that was pulled into a ponytail, and her arms were wide open, just like her smile. Surrounding her was a brightly colored bedroom that seemed to have thrown up purple. She looked to be around twelve, rail thin, but happy.

As Kirin glanced from the picture back to Gianna, she saw emotion she'd never seen. Gianna had tears in her eyes.

Steve reached over and touched Gianna's hand and to Kirin's surprise, Gianna didn't flinch or even pull away.

"It took a long time and a lot of red tape, but she's finally officially adopted. She's mine and she's home."

Kirin handed back the photo and nodded.

Gianna sucked in a deep breath and shakily exhaled before continuing. "Here's the problem, I made Paloma a promise to find her fifteen-year-old sister, Arianna, who was also sold."

"And…"

Gianna twisted uncomfortably in her seat. "Well, since I'm still attending the hearings to exonerate myself from Nicky's death, I couldn't go after her myself."

Kirin waited for the verdict she already knew.

"Sam and I made a deal."

"What deal?" Kirin could feel the heat rising up the back of her neck.

"Sam would go after her and bring her back."

Kirin waited a beat for the rest, but Gianna just stared at her. "In exchange for what?"

"I can't tell you that."

The chair squawked as Kirin jerked to her feet. "Oh, yes you can! That's my husband you've put in harm's way."

Tears stung Kirin's eyes, but she was proud, none fell. She pointed at Steve who immediately put both hands up.

"Before you even ask, nope, I didn't know a damn thing about this cockamamie idea, or I would've stopped it. You know me better than that."

Flustered, Kirin turned back toward Gianna, who was already speaking.

"Listen. We've all been trying to find the supplier. The one who controls the runners who tag the vehicles and snatch the young women." Gianna pointed toward Kirin's front door. "You know, with I-40 and I-75 intersecting right here in Knoxville this is the prime place for runners to transport, but if we can't stop these rings from the top, we're wasting our time."

Gianna stood and paced. "It runs so deep. So political. Even moving my firm to East Tennessee and changing our primary focus hasn't helped. I have a whole team working with only the subset of girls who were promised clear passage from Mexico into the US only to find they're sold to the highest bidder as indentured servants or for sex."

As Gianna said the last word, her voice cracked.

Kirin watched her closely as she tried to compose herself and continue.

"We tracked Arianna through some of the underground spies we have all the way to Chicago—the main artery of their operation." Gianna rubbed her face. "Sam wasn't supposed to go off grid. He was supposed to be meeting with one of our people and negotiating with…"

Gianna trailed off. She wouldn't look at Kirin.

Kirin still stood.

"With whom?"

Gianna didn't answer. She stared at her hands folded in front of her and wouldn't meet Kirin's gaze.

Kirin slammed her fist on the table, making Gianna's gaze snap to hers.

"Who?"

Gianna exhaled.

"Detroit Mafia, Chicago branch."

Chapter Five

When door number five opened, a demure woman appeared with a gentle face and eyes that kissed in the corners. She looked to be about seventy-five, with wrinkled coffee-colored skin and bare feet. She smiled, nodded, and waved for them to step inside.

At first, the suite appeared dark. Rosa's eyes adjusted quickly, and she could make out three pleather orange couches arranged in a U pattern, with a small table in the middle. Beyond that was a swath of green fake grass with a golf tee in the middle of it and at the back of the small room was a large screen, backlit with a lime green light.

Low voices, in a language she didn't know, wafted over the half wall from the adjoining bay. RD pointed toward the orange couch and walked toward it. When her niece sat on the edge, she bowed her head, much like the broken girls Rosa had seen and quite frankly, been herself, growing up.

Kirin's Dad, Sonny, had been the one to save her and here she was handing over her beautiful niece.

Rosa caught movement in the corner of the room. A house of a man, dressed all in black, stood like a statue next to the screen. She hadn't seen him when she'd first scanned the room, but she was grateful now that neither she nor RD had broken character.

He lifted both arms, slowly as if he was mechanical, and lit a cigarette. The orange glow was all that she could see, but when he went to take a drag, the glow illuminated the lower half of his face. She could've been mistaken, but slow like the Grinch, a sinister sneer crept across his lips. Something about his stance seemed expectant and giddy as if he was going to enjoy whatever happened next.

After a beat, the voices in the other bay rose from low and conversational to heated. No...jovial. Almost as if they were watching a soccer match. Their voices rose and fell and at the end erupted in laughter and applause.

It was then dimmed lights turned on in the suite.

Three men, laughing, walked from the bay next door to the one where they sat waiting. A younger man was first to come into view flanked by two older men.

Then Rosa saw the one thing she hoped she wouldn't see.

Chapter Six

Gianna knew it took everything in Kirin's strong will not to slap her across the face.

It was one thing to ask Sam, her best friend and ex, to go on a dangerous mission two weeks before their wedding. Even for her, that was pretty shitty. But the Detroit Mafia was several levels higher on the danger meter.

Gianna straightened her top, pulling her face back ever so slightly so that she was just out of Kirin's reach. Unless of course she lunged across the table, which, at this point Gianna wouldn't blame her one bit. Or put it past her for that matter.

She had to try and make her understand.

"Listen. I know. I know those people are crazy and dangerous and the last thing I wanted was to put anyone I love in harm's way."

Kirin rolled her eyes. *Yeah, she deserved that.*

Steve, for his part, held on to her hand way too long sending unwelcome warmth into her arms that she knew she didn't deserve, but needed like air. She couldn't bring herself to pull away.

Gianna continued, "But, we can't discount the fact that we still don't know who is calling the shots and we must stop the influx of girls being transported against their will under the guise that they'll be free. Steve can tell you; they've been tracking a group for months and all roads lead back to the Detroit Clan."

Steve released her hand and spoke to Kirin.

"We intercepted another truck load just two nights ago. It's just sad. These are just kids, and not only Hispanic kids, but girls from poor households and wealthy households, and a few girls who thought they were meeting boys from Snap Chat at the mall.

Some of these girls were dressed up to look like hookers. But the one thing they had in common, all of them were scared. Listen, I know. Sam promised you no more missions, but this one, albeit ill advised," Steve added, pinning Gianna with his gaze, "sounds as if it had merit and a chance to work. But now that he's gone off grid, I think it's fair to say that he's been seized."

Steve had captured the conversation and for that Gianna was grateful.

Gianna took a deep breath and added, "And there's only one thing we can do."

When Kirin asked, "What?" Gianna picked at her fingernails for a beat before answering. She'd need to tell her just enough, so she'd buy in, but not everything.

When Gianna explained *part* of her plan, Kirin's horrified expression told her it was the worst idea in the history of ideas.

Then, Kirin sat with her head in her hands for a few minutes. Obviously struggling with what to do next.

Eventually, Kirin glanced up, and pinned Gianna with her gaze.

After a beat, she nodded.

She'd come to the same conclusion Gianna had.

They had no choice.

Chapter Seven

RD hadn't planned for this.

Her intel had indicated that the man she sought was old, fat, Asian and not in the best health. A smoker, who coughed a lot with a gravelly voice. She figured, if nothing else, she could defend herself against someone slow and ill. She strategically bent her head but watched everything in the dimly lit room through the curls in her fake hair.

But the man who strutted around the corner, wasn't old or fat. He was a well-dressed, young Asian man, tough, and full on handsome with a strong southern voice and piercing eyes that looked as if they'd crumble anyone.

She also hadn't planned for two other men, and the third larger bouncer with a permanent scowl who stood in the corner staring through her as if he could read her mind.

She tried not to look anyone in the eye but did manage to get an eyeful of the young man in front before lowering her gaze back down to the floor. Her research and recon had told her that the older girls who were taken were significantly more brain washed than the younger girls. Older ones, if not brainwashed, will fight harder where the younger girls are so terrified, they mainly just want the whole thing over with.

He'd been laughing as he rounded the corner. He must've been the one playing the video game. He tugged on a grey suit jacket over his peach-colored tailored shirt. The skin on his hands was a beautiful brown and his hair was shiny and black, looking recently coiffed into a Tom Cruise cut. His shirt seemed a bit tight across the chest and arms, which told her that he wasn't stick thin as the other two. He'd be harder to fight if it came to that, but she knew instantly from his demeanor, he was the boss in the room and exactly for whom she'd been waiting.

Even in the dimmed lights, she saw the hilt of his gun sticking out the back of his trousers when he tugged on the jacket. Not good, especially when hers was wrapped tightly around her ankle.

When the room got quiet, she stared only at the floor. RD sensed the younger man's eyes on her. He sat slowly directly across from her on the couch, while the other two stood behind him. She could've just as easily imagined him plopping down like a kid. He sat on the edge of the orange couch, legs bent, yet spread wide and his hands clasped lightly together. He didn't say a word as he sized up both she and her aunt.

RD knew exactly the fresh hell that her aunt had been through during her lifetime. She'd been told the stories since birth. She'd been sold into slavery at a very young age. Made to do unspeakable things, then saved by a man she didn't even know.

Her Tia had fought and scraped for everything she had, then used the last few years of her life repaying the favor by taking care of the man's daughter and her kids.

In RD's opinion, still acting like a servant.

But she also knew that her aunt was tough and resilient and had dealt with her fair share of scumbags like this privileged, confident prick sitting across from her. And she had the acting chops to pull this off.

RD just hoped her aunt wouldn't hesitate. She needed to make the deal and leave. That was the agreement.

Now, the dance could begin.

~*~

Rosa stared right back at the overconfident, overdressed pinhead. If anything, her years of experience gained her an edge and she understood the assignment, but she was afraid when it came right down to walking out that door without her niece—leaving her own blood behind with these monsters— she wasn't entirely sure she could pull it off.

Finally, with a half-smile that didn't touch his eyes, he snatched a short glass with light amber liquid inside that rested on the table, sat back as if he was about to watch a movie, took a sip, then spoke, "Stand and turn."

Rosa almost stood before she realized the young man was talking to her niece and not her.

Old habits.

RD stood, still staring at the floor, and turned, then quickly sat.

The young man stared at RD for a beat, eyebrows knitted together. Quickly, he placed his drink back on the table between them and snapped his fingers. RD glanced up, locking eyes with him.

The young man's head turned slightly to the side, like a dog hearing a whistle. He crooked a finger at her, and she scooted forward on the couch so that her knees were touching the small coffee table that separated them. He reached out and pulled her chin up, to get a good look at her face.

Rosa saw a slight flash of something in his eyes. Recognition, maybe? Anyone else might have missed it, but Rosa didn't.

God, she hoped not. With RD's face still in his grasp, he held her still, smiling slightly as if he knew something she didn't. He pinned RD inside his gaze as he asked a question.

"Bi-lingual or Tri?"

"Bi," Rosa answered for her.

"Not virginal?"

Rosa cocked her head to one side, "At twenty-five would you be?"

He glanced over and smiled at Rosa, shook his head, and then looked back at RD, his fingers released her chin and instead found purchase touching a lock of her hair. He twirled it with his fingertips, never taking his eyes off her niece.

"Take your shirt off," he commanded.

Rosa scoffed and lowered her voice to a growl, "No, absolutely no free shows. Where's my money?"

But to her horror, RD stood quickly and whisked off her shirt, staring at the ground. Her black sports bra looked worn in a few places and Rosa knew it had to be one of her favorites.

The young man carefully took his glass and sat back on the couch again. He took a small pull of whatever was in the glass and motioned with one finger for RD to turn.

Rosa knew her eyes were downcast, so she commanded her to turn, and RD complied.

She was grateful to see that her niece hadn't stashed her gun in her waistband or else the whole room would've seen it.

The man took his time, watching and it made Rosa sick. She knew they were trying to pull something out of her, make her break to ensure she wasn't police.

Setting his drink back on the table, he raised one arm and made a motion with his hand. When he did the people in the room all moved as if they'd heard a silent whistle. All scurried out the door, except for the ninja looking man in the corner.

Within seconds the two men and the older woman were out, and the door clicked shut.

The younger man turned his head slowly to look at the person in all black in the shadowed corner. Then he said something in what Rosa could only imagine was Chinese. It sounded gruff and harsh like he was giving the man orders. The man in the corner said nothing. He shook his head, tamped out his cigarette on the putting green like he owned the place, whispered something in the younger man's ear, then left.

When the door finally shut, the young man stood abruptly, tearing off his suit jacket and forcefully rolling up his sleeves. Rosa watched him. He was angry. She'd never seen anyone switch emotions that rapidly.

What happened next went so fast, she had no warning and zero ability to stop it.

Chapter Eight

Early Saturday morning Kirin was an absolute hot mess. Her mind flitted from one problem to the next like an erratic butterfly landing on hot lava.

After dropping Will off at a friend's house for the weekend with a friend from middle school and Little Jack, who at eight wasn't so little anymore, off with her Aunt Kathy and Uncle Dean, Kirin tried her hardest not to think about Sam and what the Detroit Mafia might do to him.

She tried not to think of their last night together. The way he'd held her and made her feel like nothing could break their bond. They'd laughed at how they'd met over a mound of tomatoes, how she'd been so stubborn and fallen into trouble more than anyone he'd ever protected. And how on the exterior he'd been so confident and strong, but inside had felt like a thirteen-year-old boy when he'd confessed how much he'd loved her for the first time.

That conversation and the feeling of safety now seemed like weeks ago. Since then, she'd paced, cried, and not slept but a few fitful hours.

She refused to allow her mind to picture her life without Sam if they decided to kill him. She'd had to do that before, and she was unwilling to do it again.

She knew firsthand what kind of monsters they were. They cared only about three things: money, drug shipments, and truckloads of girls to abduct and sell.

Nope. She was not going to think that way. She'd occupy her mind with the last two things on her wedding checklist. It felt useless—like rearranging chairs on the Titanic, but Kirin was choosing to be positive, and she'd have to finish as if there would still be a wedding.

Gianna, Steve, and the bomb that had been dropped on her the night before flashed into her memory. Gianna was out of her damn mind if she thought Kirin was going to trust her with this stupid see-through plan. And the worst part was that Steve seemed completely on board with this suicide mission.

Kirin shook her head as she parked her car.

She had an agenda of her own. Saturday mornings always involved visiting Laura first thing in the rehab facility. Mornings were the best time to drag a few clues out of her friend.

Laura had only been out of the coma for a few months and truly, she'd come so far, but her mind was still spotty, resetting every couple of minutes like Groundhog Day and even worse, her sense of what was real and what was imaginary was skewed. The doctors had warned them that these hallucinations were normal as her brain was still adjusting and the swelling was going away, albeit slower than they would've liked.

When Kirin arrived, Adam was standing in her doorway, backing away, yet yelling back into Laura's room. Kirin froze a foot from him.

"I told you! That never happened. That's one of those things the doc said your mind is making up. I did not have an affair with— oh, thank God, Kirin's here. Please tell your friend that I did not have an affair with someone at my job."

Adam's arms flailed and his face was beet red. He was the epitome of a chunky husband, completely in love with his wife who'd never once entertained the idea of straying. But Laura's mind was convinced that something she'd dreamed was real.

This was where it got hard.

Kirin raised her eyebrows at Adam, then put on a good smiling face and rounded the corner. Laura seemed to forget her anger from just a few seconds before and smiled when she saw her friend.

Laura's gate and speech were still slow and some of her fine motor skills were hit or miss. Lying on top of her hospital covers, she wore grey sweats and a black T-shirt, both of which hung on her bony frame. Her eyes seemed clear and bright today. Maybe today would be a better visit than last time.

When Kirin was close enough, Laura held up both arms and they embraced. Adam was smart enough to back completely out of the room and take a walk. Laura rolled her eyes as he left.

"Has he?" Laura asked, pointing at the door.

"Has he, what?"

"Cheated?"

Kirin took a hard look at her friend. "What's your gut say?"

Laura stared at the ceiling for a beat, then answered. "No. He's right. That had to be a dream. It's getting so hard to tell what's real." Laura turned to Kirin and grabbed both her hands.

"You know this is all my fault, right?"

Kirin sighed. *Groundhog Day.* "Honey, we've been over this. The blast was not your fault."

Laura released her hands and quickly pushed her body higher in the bed.

"Yes it was. I was working with the URS and triaging the girls who'd been rescued before sending them down the line to be reunited with their families. I worked with another young man who was a therapist and who tried his hardest to convince these brainwashed girls they were going home to families that loved and missed them. My job was tough, but his was worse."

Kirin's ears perked up. She'd heard the same stories over and over, but this was the first mention of another person on the inside who could help.

"What was his name?" Kirin asked.

"Whose?" Laura answered.

"The therapist?"

"I'm not sure. We never exchanged information, we just used our code to get into this tiny underground apartment and started working."

New information. Kirin made mental notes.

"Where was the apartment again?" Kirin had asked this question many times but usually it was right when her friend's brain got tired, and she never was able to tell her.

Laura rolled her eyes and grabbed for her water cup and straw. Kirin patiently helped her, knowing the straw was the bane of her existence. She couldn't quite get it into her mouth without some help.

After Laura gulped, she answered, "I've told you a thousand times, underneath Mast General Store, downtown."

Kirin thought quickly, "Which apartment?"

"B-4, but be careful, the code is tricky. It's 37918#, but if you mess up, an alarm will go off and you'll need to leave, quickly. And remember the password is *pickles*."

Laura squeezed her eyes and shook her head. "Sounds like espionage. That's gotta be one of the things my mind made up, right? Or like the plot to one of those Jason Bourne movies?"

Kirin had made a pact not to lie to Laura. She owed her friend that.

"No, honey, that one is real. You were a badass before the blast."

Both women smiled.

"Kirin?"

"Hmm?"

"You know, Sam isn't all bad, right?"

Kirin nodded.

"But I think D'Angelo is going to kill him."

Kirin's heart dropped in her stomach, but she kept calm.

"And D'Angelo is who?" Kirin's voice cracked a little as she scooted to the edge of her seat.

Laura yawned big, which was normally her brain's signal that their conversation was coming to an end, and she needed to rest.

As her friend scootched down in her bed and closed her eyes, she said words that gave Kirin chills up her spine.

"Detroit Mafia in Chicago."

Then she fell asleep.

Chapter Nine

Rosa wanted to scream.

How could this have gone so badly so quickly? She stood in the hallway in pain, breathing heavy with a stack of cash large enough that her hand couldn't close around it. Her purse hung off one forearm, her finger throbbed and the strap on her shoe had snapped.

Because before she could've said a word, that idiot had thrown off his jacket, rolled up his sleeves, and pulled his gun, pointing it directly in Rosa's face.

RD, for her part, didn't even look up.

Rosa had raised her arms slowly and glared at the man.

"Double cross?" she'd asked in perfect Spanish, trying to stay in character. Then in English, "Where's my money?"

The younger man slapped a stack of cash in her hand, spun her around and literally shoved her out the door so hard that she stumbled into the wall. Her shoe broke and she jammed her finger trying to break her fall.

She stood for a quick second, remembered what RD had told her and ran for the elevator. With a shaky hand she pushed the down button. She felt helpless and empty. She had to resist the urge to run back upstairs, use the tiny gun in her purse and rescue her niece.

They were doing the right thing. They'd talked it over and over and she knew this was the only way to find the supplier. The FBI had tried several tactics, but all were thwarted. Undercover was the only way and RD had been trained by the best.

She refused to cry until she got out of there. Cameras were everywhere and if they saw any emotion, it would blow her niece's cover and ruin everything.

Rosa had agreed to embark on this journey. Now she hoped they both hadn't bitten off more than they could chew.

~*~

When he'd shoved her aunt out the door and locked it, RD wanted to punch the guy in the face. As it was, she'd have to ride out whatever happened next. Most of the research she'd done indicated that she'd either be beaten or raped. Her new captor would need to show dominance and she'd need to take it. She'd prepared herself either way.

Through gritted teeth, he commanded, "Look at me."

She obeyed.

Alarm bells went off in her mind. Something seemed too familiar about the way he spoke and how he looked. His dark eyes searched hers as if she was missing something that he could see.

Angrily, he stalked around her like a cat, sweat beading slightly at his temples. He couldn't have been more than a year older than her. Her stomach twisted. It appeared she might have to endure both horrible things she'd heard about.

Without warning, the man took two steps and shoved the table between them out of the way.

His chest was inches from her face. She could smell the expensive cologne on his unwrinkled shirt. She catalogued the smell, trying to calm her mind.

"What the hell do you think you're doing?" He whispered hoarsely as he shoved the pistol down the back of his pants.

RD didn't answer. She was caught in the hazy familiarity of his face.

He lowered his gaze, "Don't move or I swear to God, I'll hurt you." His body dipped down, shoving her ankles apart, he roughly lifted the cuff of her jeans and ripped the Velcro holster holding her gun. When he pulled it loose, he stood, unloaded the magazine, pulled the one out of the chamber and shoved it all in a small black carryon bag she hadn't noticed in the corner of the room.

When he stalked back over, he stood toe to toe with her.

"Did you honestly think I wouldn't recognize you?" He ran his hands through his hair and something inside her clicked.

RD's mouth went dry, but her face stayed constant.

Jesus, who was this guy?

He looked familiar. *Shit.* She'd already blown this. Whoever he was, he seemed to know her even with disguise.

And now, she didn't even have her weapon.

She was gonna have to fight her way out of this one.

Chapter Ten

After seeing Laura in the hospital and Kirin's final wedding dress fitting—the dress she'd probably never get to wear, she drove downtown and parked.

Kirin's mind flitted to the night before. Gianna had held something back in her kitchen. Something in her gut said if she was gonna get Sam back, she'd need all the information, not just part of it.

Sam would be pissed if he knew she was taking this risk, but she had no choice. The only way to get the intel she needed, was to go herself.

Kirin locked her car and found the first set of massive concrete stairs at the base of the bridge. She cinched her purse and started down them.

In the early part of the 20th century, when cars were just becoming all the rage, downtown Knoxville embarked on a massive construction project aimed at leveling out the dangerous, steep mountain roads. Massive inclines and declines around downtown were causing an alarming number of accidents.

Their MPC decided that the only solution would be to build the road up and even it out, essentially making some of the first few floors of several buildings *underneath* the main road in the city.

Today, the hip young urbanites that were moving downtown were shocked to find that the ground level of the shops was the 4th floor in most of the old buildings.

About halfway down the concrete steps, she came to an abrupt halt. Two homeless men were camped out on one of the landings, still too early to rise, as the sun hadn't hit that far down just yet.

Kirin crept around them like a child playing hide and seek, tiptoeing on the edge so she didn't step on the dirty, worn blanket or the foot of the other one who slept peacefully under a jacket draped over his shoulders. She wondered if some kind stranger had done this while they were asleep.

At the bottom of the stairs she faced two sets of glass doors surrounded by brick. Neither door had any markings on it. She searched her memory. Had Laura said which one? Nope. She'd have to choose and pray she didn't look like someone who was trying to break in.

The door on the left had a package outside of it as if the UPS guy had just left it.

For some reason, that door felt more like families lived there. So, she walked toward the door on the right. She'd worn her regular scrubs today, for two reasons. She prayed she'd made a good decision there.

A black keypad was embedded into the wall. Kirin took a deep breath. She pressed, #37918.

Piercing, angry, unstoppable beeps indicated she'd input it wrong. She stepped back and her fingers started to tremble. Either she'd messed up, or she was at the wrong door. Nonetheless, she needed to fix it fast as she was in danger, and she knew it.

Shaking out her fingers, she lifted her hand to try again. Wait…Laura had said 37918 then the pound sign. She'd input it backwards.

Quickly, she typed in 37918# and the beeping stopped. As soon as the beeping stopped, she heard a buzzing at the base of the door and lunged for it.

It opened with a click into a damp and dark hallway. From somewhere inside she heard a dog barking. Probably in response to the dang alarm going off.

As her eyes adjusted, she noticed some of the numbers on the doors had long since fallen off and were written on with a sharpie.

"B-1, B-2, B-3…and B-4." She whispered.

Standing at the door, she took a deep breath and knocked. Nothing.

No noise, no shuffling around as she would've expected. It was as if she'd come on the wrong day. But she knew Laura had mentioned that she helped every Saturday before the blast.

Maybe they'd replaced her and were now suspicious of the woman at the door. Or maybe this was just another dead end.

Kirin knocked once more, only this time, she heard the shuffling of feet as if her knock startled whoever was peeking at her through the peephole.

Three clicks indicated that someone was unlocking the deadbolts. She held her breath.

When a young man opened the door only a crack and stared at her with a look that screamed distrust, she moved closer, whispering. "Laura sent me. I'm a nurse. May I come in and help?"

The man's brow furrowed deeper, "Don't know a Laura." He said and began to push the door closed.

Kirin quickly stuck her foot in the crack in the door with both hands on it. "Wait! Pickles. I was supposed to say Pickles. I'm sorry, I forgot that part."

The young man exhaled. His shoulders dropped slightly. "Put your ID through the door."

Kirin dug in her purse. Laura didn't tell her this part. She handed over her ID and the man scanned it and her as he held the door tight. Kirin didn't move her foot, for fear he'd lock it and she'd never get it back.

Finally, he passed the ID back to her, opened the door only slightly more and motioned for her to skinny her way through it.

When she emerged on the other side, she completely understood why the door couldn't open.

Beside him, stood a tiny old woman with a kind face, holding a gun.

It was the oddest-looking thing. She looked as if she could bake cookies and read stories, yet she held the gun as if she knew exactly how to kill a human and had done so in the past.

Kirin's hands immediately went up.

The young man glanced at Kirin, puzzled, then followed her line of sight, whispered something to the woman and she lowered the gun and shuffled away.

The apartment was dimly lit with no windows, cramped with too much old furniture, and the smell was a cross between a musty basement and someone burning bread. Sitting on the couch were three girls, all clinging to each other, terrified. They held one another as if they'd been friends since birth. Maybe they would be now that they'd been rescued.

The young man crooked a finger at Kirin, and she followed him down a dark hall. The first door on the right was a bedroom that had been transformed into a triage point. Laura was meticulous in her organization at work, so she knew this had once been her spot. Gauze, BP cuff, tape, irrigation tools, prescribed bruise and cut meds, as well as butterfly enclosures and sutures, lined one long counter, while a chair sat in the middle.

In the chair was a dark-headed girl, looking as if she was being held against her will. She gripped the arms of the chair and stared at Kirin and the man as if they were the bad people.

It was then Kirin noticed her hands were zip tied to the chair.

When she put her purse in the corner, she glanced up at the young man, who was pulling another chair closer to her. Kirin shot him a questioning look that he ignored. In a soothing voice, he spoke to the room.

"Now that you're calm, let's talk about the situation."

"You untie me right now or I'm going to scream until the police come."

The young man steepled his hands. "I've already told you. You're safe. We're the people who are going to get you back to your family. You've been rescued."

"I didn't *ask* to be rescued, you twit." She spat as she thrashed around in her chair.

In the face, the girl looked to be about fifteen. She had thick, dark hair that was put up in a long pony that cascaded halfway down her back and curled at the ends. Immediately Kirin noticed a tattoo on her shoulder. She was way too young for that.

Her eyes were a cross between cocoa and pine, the deepest of hazel, and her lips full and pink. She was a beauty, and obviously a spitfire, but her speech and the way she was dressed made her appear more like a young adult than a kid.

The man who spoke to her kept his tone even and his face soft and kind, even as she began to thrash around.

"I told you, all we want is to save you from the people who took you. This lady here is just going to dress the cut on your arm."

The girl's angry gaze spun around, she stilled and glared at Kirin. "Touch me and I'll beat your ass."

Kirin stared at the girl for a beat, then decided how to play it. She lowered her face even with the girl's and put on her mama voice. The same one Will always called her, "*She-means-business voice.*"

"You're just gonna have to beat my ass then, 'cause that cut," Kirin pointed, and the girl looked down, "is infected. And I'm a nurse and a mom who's not gonna let you lose your arm."

The girl stilled when Kirin turned back to the counter, gathered her supplies, then stomped toward her like a mama bear. Kirin shot her a look that said don't move and began irrigating her wound.

The girl watched Kirin's hands as if she were learning how to crochet. Every flick of Kirin's fingers first irrigating the wound, checking for signs of infection, applying the antibiotic cream that would hopefully put a halt to any infection trying to attack her arm, and finally applying gauze and tape, carefully and with the softest of touches.

For a moment, their gazes locked. In that one look Kirin saw a little girl, lost and forgotten. It was as if her *thank you* was giving Kirin a glimpse into who she really was. Tough on the outside and scared on the inside. When Kirin shot her a tight smile, the young girl returned it.

Young *Mr. Rogers* began again with his calming voice, trying to strike while the girl was at least still and allowing them to help.

"Your captors convinced you they cared about you, but they didn't. They saw you for what they could use you for. Your loyalty to them is textbook Stockholm Syndrome. Were you taken from your family?"

The girl's gaze flitted from Kirin to the young man. She looked for just a second as if whatever he was saying was beginning to get through her tough exterior.

The girl nodded.

As he continued to speak with her, she began to cry. Kirin gathered up all the trash from the packages she'd opened and quietly slipped out of the room, not wanting to break the spell.

She padded into the kitchen to see the kindly older woman cooking eggs. She held up her hands with the trash inside and the elder woman smiled and pointed her spatula toward a trashcan in the corner.

After Kirin had quickly triaged the other three girls, who obviously hadn't been in the system long and didn't need medical care, she sat with them for several minutes until the older woman placed food on the table.

The girls looked uneasy as if they weren't sure who to trust. Kirin herded them toward the table and even took a bite of their food, to ensure them nothing funny was going on.

The three ate as if it was their last meal.

Just then, a thud, crash, and a scream from the first door on the right froze them all.

Within seconds a blur ran down the hall, knocking past Kirin and to the door before she could even get her arms out to stop her. Wild hazel eyes, glaring, pinned her as she ran past. Before the old woman or any of them could stop the young girl, she had the three deadbolts unhooked and the door flung open.

The last Kirin saw of her was her pony tail swishing as she darted around the corner.

Kirin dropped her fork and chased the girl into the dark hallway. By the time she got around the corner, the girl was at the glass door leading to the street.

"Hey!"

Kirin yelled, startling the girl enough to make her stop.

"We're trying to help you."

In true teenager fashion, the girl responded, "I don't need your help." Then she flipped Kirin off and vanished.

Kirin heard the click of another door opening because of her voice, and she dove back into B-4, shutting and locking the door back.

~*~

"I'd lock the knives and scalpels up next time, if I were you." Kirin said offhand as she dressed the wound in the man's upper thigh.

"She was good. Best I've seen so far, and I've seen some doozies. But that right there, that was a spy."

Kirin's hands froze.

"Why do you think that?"

"Didn't she seem a little too confident to you?"

Kirin thought for a second as she placed the last bit of tape on the gauze covering his gash.

"Maybe just spirited. I thought it might help her regain who she was."

"Stockholm makes them certain everyone else is crazy and they're right. Makes them think that their captor truly loves them. But it doesn't usually present in confidence like that. Conviction, yes, confidence, no."

Kirin nodded.

In truth, the young girl reminded Kirin of Gianna when she'd first met her. Headstrong, foul mouthed, cockiness. And full of it.

When they finished, the man stood, clearly favoring the leg. "Get that checked out, Monday at the latest, K?"

He nodded.

Now was her chance, "I need some help."

He was placing chairs right side up and cleaning all the tools the girl had knocked over and he stopped mid grab, glanced up at her, wary.

"Do you know the process once a girl is taken?"

He watched her carefully, obviously trying to determine if she, too, was a spy.

"Don't you?" He asked.

"Not really."

The man began cleaning up a bit faster, probably wanting her out of the apartment.

Laura had obviously trusted him. Kirin should too.

"Can I be honest with you?" He stopped again, sizing her up, nodding. "My future husband went up to Chicago yesterday to try and rescue a specific girl."

The man's eyebrows shot up.

"Right? Complete suicide attempt if you ask me. But my problem is that he's gone off the grid and we can't locate him. I need to know what happens when the girls are taken. Maybe something in that info will help me figure out where they're holding him, if…"

Kirin trailed off. She didn't want to think about if he was still alive. No. Not going there. She realized she was twisting the towel she had in her hand and released it.

The younger man stared at her a beat, then spoke.

"As I understand it, they usually fly to Chicago, unless it's a special circumstance. At that point, they could go anywhere. A couple of girls have mentioned a penthouse in a tall building, but that could describe anywhere.

"They're met by someone at a touristy place and transported for auction. I'm sorry, I wish I knew more."

Kirin thanked him, said she'd return the following Saturday, then said goodbye to the older woman and hugged the girls before walking out the door.

On the way back to her car, her mind spun, but she kept an eye out for the girl, hoping to catch up with her and talk.

But that one was long gone.

~*~

A few hours later, after lunch, Kirin reluctantly pulled into the parking lot of the most torturous establishment on the planet.

She shook away the memory of the underground apartment, the headstrong girl, and the counselor. She had a bigger problem at hand.

Her hands shook as she pulled her keys out of the ignition and sat in the quiet for a moment.

The devil herself, wearing designer sunglasses and a peach-colored pants suit leaned up against her convertible staring at Kirin in her car. When Kirin didn't move, the wench tapped her watch.

Put this on the long list of idiotic things a woman does to save the man she loves.

Kirin tossed her purse in the floorboard and locked the doors. Gianna looked positively giddy, but with a question in her eyes.

"I'm not bringing my purse. You're paying for this." Kirin stated plainly.

Gianna nodded and gestured for Kirin to go first, then added, "Don't you own anything other than scrubs?"

Kirin stopped in her tracks and turned to stare at Gianna.

"You really want to do this now?"

Gianna, for her part, looked remorsefully downward. "You're right. I'm sorry."

"Can we please record that so that I can play it back on repeat over the next few hellish days?" Kirin asked as she brushed past Gianna up the steps.

Kirin took a deep breath before pulling open the heavy glass door. Walking through, her senses were subtly assaulted. Soft piano music played in the background and the smell of fresh cut flowers and hair dye attacked Kirin's nose. The woman at the desk had her hair up in an elaborate bun that looked like she was getting married. She was tan and toned and wore a long, sleeveless sundress, as if she were going to a party on a yacht. She took a long look at Kirin. Her voice dripped in what appeared to be a fake French accent.

"Welcome. Your name, madame?"

When Gianna waltzed in behind Kirin a second later, a boisterous, well-groomed man came sweeping up from somewhere in the back holding two flutes of champagne.

"G!" he trilled. "We're so delighted to have you back!" He handed one glass to Gianna and one to Kirin, barely acknowledging Kirin's presence as he fawned all over the wench.

Gianna went straight into debutant mode. "Hello Frederick. Thank you so much for taking us in with such a short notice." She took a sip of her champagne as Kirin just stared at her.

Frederick answered, "When my best client tells me she needs a favor, I jump." As he was talking, his hands went into Kirin's hair. She froze like a deer in the woods.

"I see." He said, eyebrows furrowed, concentrating on Kirin's mid-length recently washed, box store bought blonde locks.

"I have the perfect idea. Follow me, ladies."

Kirin had a very bad feeling about this.

Chapter Eleven

The Asian man took a step back from RD, crossed his arms and sized her up. His face registered disbelief as if he was waiting for something.

"Were you really that drunk?"

RD fought to remain staring blankly ahead as her mind raced. *Oh no*. She'd partaken in some hefty drinking recently. But no more than her fellow FBI cadets. Maybe a few times too many. But only once had she ended up doing the walk of shame home the next morning.

That's when her memory snapped.

It was Halloween. Her class of cadets had decided to go to a local bar and have a beer in costume. The only catch was they all had to draw costume ideas from a jar.

She'd, of course, chosen the worst—a pregnant nun.

All the ideas were bad, but that one, with her Catholic upbringing, was awful. And to top it off, the bet was she couldn't score a guy in a pregnant nun outfit.

Thanks to some shots at the bar, she'd found one. Dressed like an old-time bandit with a black and white striped pajamas and a mask made from a black sock.

He'd looked like he'd lost a bet too.

Turned out, he was intelligent and funny. Cute too, but that could've just been the shots. They'd talked and laughed and drank for hours. Then he ghosted her.

But this couldn't be him. No way. That guy was laid back and fun. Same height, but nothing else seemed to be dinging bells. If she could stare into his eyes, she'd know if it was him, but right now she had to stay in character and stare straight ahead at his neck to survive.

"I'm sorry. I don't know what you're talking about." She said and cast her gaze back to the floor.

He shook his head, then started gathering his things.

"That's how you wanna play it? Fine. Just remember, you set this thing in motion, I didn't." he said, sharply. She cut her eyes up briefly to watch him as he grabbed up his jacket and shrugged it back on.

Once he had his things and snatched up his black bag, he grabbed her forcibly by the forearm yanking her body toward his. Her face was inches from his chest. His cologne smelled familiar and did things to her resolve. The hair on her arms stood on end like he was a magnet.

He shook his head as if he was grappling internally with something, then spoke. She stared at his mouth, which was close enough that she could feel his warm breath wash over her face.

"Watch yourself. These people aren't playing a game. They're out for blood. I have an appointment but at first light you'll go through processing. Tomorrow afternoon, we leave. My advice to you is sleep. You're gonna need it."

Her belly did a quick backflip, but this time, not from fear.

"Where are we going?" she asked.

"You'll see." He answered and then stomped across the hall, unlocked a door, and shoved her inside.

The door clicked and she was all alone in the dark.

Chapter Twelve

Four hours.

Jesus, Mary, and Joseph.

Four hours later. Her own children wouldn't have recognized her. Heck, she didn't even recognize herself.

Kirin had been cut, colored, tanned, waxed, primped, pulled, primed, and poked. She had magnetic eyelashes, penciled dark eyebrows, brown contacts, dragon nails and mahogany tinted brown extensions in her hair and to top it all off, bangs for God's sake.

And God alone knew who she was.

Gianna had even brought outfits and made Kirin change into them. *Nice outfits,* Gianna kept reminding her.

Thanks to her boobs seemingly growing overnight, or Gianna giving her tops that were two sizes too small, Kirin looked like a hooker.

For the hundredth time Kirin heard herself ask, "Is all this really necessary?" To which Gianna would nod without looking up while combing the newspaper and sipping more of the expensive bubbly.

When Kirin walked out, fully clothed from her skintight shirt to leather pants and pumps that made her almost as tall as Gianna, she caught a glimpse of the finished product and stopped to stare.

She looked ridiculous.

Gianna, for what it was worth, looked stunned.

"Wow." Was all that she could say. Mouth open.

Frederick looked tired, but proud.

Gianna swallowed hard when they told her the cost, but handed over a golden card and within minutes, they were driving Kirin's car back to her house.

God, she hoped Rosa wasn't there. That would be awkward.

~*~

After dropping her car off, making calls to ensure the boys were taken care of for the next few days and dodging the Rosa bullet, thank God, Kirin and Gianna drove for the airport.

McGhee Tyson had undergone a multimillion-dollar renovation since the last time Kirin had been chased in the airport by two of the mob's hitmen, Nicky and Babyface.

It now looked more like a mall. Two stories of high-end retail establishments loomed out toward a wide aisle that snaked and turned for what felt like miles. The sheer size of the refurbished airport had doubled. The food court was larger than the rest of the place itself and it held every type of food you could imagine.

Gianna parked and turned to Kirin.

"Listen, Katy, we—"

"Katy? Who you callin' Katy?" Kirin asked, sounding as if she should've had a head bob and a sneer with her questions. Her head automatically cocked sideways as if her appearance had changed her voice.

"Oh my gosh, that's perfect! Except I need it a little more northern sounding in your voice."

Gianna grinned as she leaned toward the backseat and grabbed a small black purse, tossing it onto Kirin's lap.

Kirin opened it and peeked inside. It was filled with items she'd never seen before.

Like a brush, gum, perfume, tissues, wallet and what appeared to be an old black radio with matching black air pods. Kirin grabbed her real purse and pulled a few things out of it, adding them to the new black one. First were her glasses, some extra cash she had hidden and a handwritten note from Sam.

The last thing she'd pulled from the bottom of her purse was wrapped in a paper towel. Kirin cut her gaze toward the wench. She waited until Gianna was preoccupied fixing one of her magnetic eyelashes in her mirror before quickly pulling it from her purse and shoving it deep in the other one. That was something nobody needed to see.

When Gianna glanced over at her, Kirin whipped out the wallet to examine it. Inside was an ID with the picture Frederick had taken of her just after he completed his Frankenstein project.

She wasn't even smiling.

Her new name was Katy Collins. *Good grief.*

"As I was saying," Gianna said while applying lipstick in her mirror, "I'm going to go to the ticket counter and get our flights. I know people here, but we're gonna have to be super careful. This all goes south if I can't get my gun on the plane."

"Gun??" Kirin turned and stared as if Gianna had three heads. "How the crap are you gonna get through security?"

Gianna smiled, raised one eyebrow, and opened her door.

Kirin got out, stumbled a little on the stupid-high heels she wasn't used to yet and walked like a wobbly baby deer to the back of the car.

Gianna popped the trunk where two rolling bags were packed. One was an expensive looking hard-sided, pale pink carry on that was encrusted with some sort of bling.

The other was plain, boring, and black. It didn't take a rocket scientist to know which one Gianna had picked out for Kirin.

Just for fun, Kirin reached for the pretty one. Gianna shot her a look that said, *get real.* Kirin shook her head, scoffed then grabbed the black one.

It was lighter than she expected. Then again, judging by the tiny amount of clothing Gianna had already picked out for her, whatever was inside the bag, she probably wouldn't want to wear anyway.

Gianna shut the trunk and the two women began walking toward the door. Kirin finally spoke.

"You know, you're going to have to trust me, right?"

Gianna glanced over, thoughtfully.

"I would think the problem would be you trusting me."

Kirin nodded, grinning.

"Well, that goes without saying."

Gianna's lips turned up in a rare display of pleasure.

Kirin decided to strike while the woman was at least in a good mood.

"So, what did you promise him?"

Gianna stopped in her tracks and stared at Kirin like she'd just asked to smash the woman's favorite shoes.

Gianna cleared her throat. "I realize you still see me as the enemy. But I'm not. And the less you know about all of this, the safer you are. I'm not withholding information to make it harder on you. My goal is to keep you safe."

Gianna took a free hand and pulled a strand of hair blown by the wind, out of Kirin's fake lashes. It almost felt like a caring gesture.

"There's a reason for the disguise. I didn't make you do all of this," Gianna gestured at Kirin's body, "just to make you feel awkward. You must stay in character to stay alive."

Gianna turned and pulled her pink suitcase across the crosswalk, turning once and staring at Kirin expectantly.

Kirin shook her head and followed. She believed Gianna and yet part of her mind kept saying she was following the spider into the web.

There would be consequences.

But, in the end, she had to save Sam.

All she could do was follow.

Chapter Thirteen

What felt like minutes later, after RD had tried her hardest to get a few hours' sleep on a twin mattress that filled up the tiny soundproof closet she was thrown into, her door swung open, and light poured in.

The bulky man with the scowl from the corner stood, legs wide ready for a grapple. He said nothing, only crooked one finger telling her to come to him without words.

When she was close enough, he grabbed her arm, escorting her through double doors that needed a key card, then to the second door on the right.

Ninja man watched her as he placed his key in and unlocked the door. When it was opened, he propelled her into a dark, cold room with no carpet and one lamp sitting on a desk beside a huge monitor. A hot cup of coffee sat on the desk and RD may have drooled a little bit. She prayed it was for her.

It wasn't.

Next to the door was a short stool waiting patiently in front of a grey screen.

Before her eyes could truly adjust, a woman, short and wide caught her around the arm a few seconds after she was tossed in and roughly shoved her on the stool in front of the grey screen.

"Name?" The woman said a little out of breath as she waddled back behind her computer screen.

"Rose."

"Nope," she shot back quickly as her thick fingers clicked keys at a rapid pace.

"Your new name is..." The woman hesitated, then commanded, "stand up and turn around."

Lord. RD did as she was commanded.

"Whew, girl, you got a rear on you. Hmmm. How about Candy. Yep, your new name is Candy. Them men gonna love you."

It made RD's skin crawl. This was the job though. She needed to be sold. What she really needed right now was her gun back from the unnamed man with the beautiful face and piercing eyes that she beginning to believe at some fuzzy point in her life she'd seen naked.

Flashes of recall and recognition came in waves. As much as she knew she should be figuring out a way to get the intel and get back, her mind relived a few scenes that caused warmth to run up her neck and to her cheeks.

Yep. He'd definitely seen her naked.

But there was a caring element there too. She just couldn't place it.

When *Helga* finished giving RD a new identity, she took her picture, fingerprints and entered an entirely new person into her database.

Then, RD smelled it.

Hot burning metal as if the walls of the beautiful old building were on fire.

The woman didn't seem to notice or care as she fiddled with something under her desk. RD reached out slowly and felt the closed door next to her. Cold.

When the woman popped back up, even in the dim light RD could tell she was sweating.

She pointed to a metal chair with arm rests against the far wall. RD stood and walked to the chair, sitting.

"Under the chair is a clipboard and pen, start filling the paperwork out."

When RD sat, she instantly bent over and reached for the clipboard. The person before her must've placed it upright and as close to the wall as possible because her fingers searched the darkness of the cold floor under the chair and found nothing.

RD leaned way over putting her head between her knees. Her long extensions brushed the ground as her right hand grappled around trying to find the clipboard.

Without any warning, RD screamed out.

She was pinned, effectively blocking off her air. It felt as if an elephant had sat on her lungs.

And she could do nothing about it.

Chapter Fourteen

Kirin knew that Gianna could talk a snake out of its skin, but this was just ridiculous.

Number one, every single man within thirty feet of the Delta counter was smiling at Kirin as if she'd forgotten to wear pants.

What the hell was that? Oh yeah. Dressed like a hooker.

Number two, those who weren't looking at Kirin, were gawking at Gianna leaning over the counter flirting with a young man of about thirty who wanted nothing more than to help her with whatever problem she was whispering to him.

After twenty minutes of Kirin sitting with the luggage wondering where Gianna and the young man had whisked off to, Gianna emerged, lipstick smudged and stalking back toward her looking like a big cat that just conquered its prey.

The young Delta agent swung by, winked at Gianna, grabbed both their rolling bags and without another word, he was gone.

Kirin shook her head as they walked up the ramp toward security.

"What?" Gianna asked defensively as they waited in line.

"Nothing. You just always get what you want, don't you?"

It was not necessarily a serious question, but Gianna took it that way. She thought for a moment until Kirin thought she wasn't going to answer. Then she turned and leaned toward Kirin.

"No. I don't. There are some things in this world that just aren't meant for me." Gianna glanced over at a young couple in line ahead of them. They wore matching shirts. One said, "She's my sweet potato," and the other one said, "I Yam." Trailing from the woman's backpack was a pin that read, "NEWLYWEDS."

Gianna nodded in their direction and Kirin followed her line of sight then scoffed. Because of the things she'd been made to do, she didn't feel worthy of a happy ending. A small crack of compassion in Kirin's heart opened up for her.

"What makes you think you can't have that?"

Gianna leveled a look at her as if she was delusional.

"I'm not you, *housewife*. We're not built the same."

Kirin just shrugged and looked out the same window she'd watched the planes land with Will and Little Jack the day she returned from her father's funeral.

Gianna pulled out a mirror, fixed her smudge, slapped it closed then turned toward Kirin, "Look, Miss high and mighty. What I'm doing, is saving your fiancé."

Kirin spun, eyebrows raised, "Who's in danger because of *you*."

Gianna opened her mouth and then closed it again. She nodded in agreement and for one of the first times, seemed remorseful. Kirin could feel that crack of compassion opening a little more for the woman, like it had when she'd watched Gianna run to her friend Stacy to comfort her. And when she'd effectively stood between the Detroit Mafia and two of her most favorite people—Sam and Will.

"Well, I'm gonna fix that," Gianna said, more to herself than to Kirin.

Kirin opened the black purse Gianna had given her and pointed inside.

"G, what the hell is this thing for?"

Gianna turned with an odd smile on her face, staring at Kirin like she was seeing her for the first time.

She shook her head slightly, moved up in line and then answered back over her shoulder. "Actors use them when they want to learn a new accent or dialogue."

"Great. And what am I learning?"

Gianna grinned, "Didn't you read your license? You're from Jersey."

~*~

As much as she'd really hated the homely housewife in the past, either finally getting a daughter had softened her or Kirin was starting to grow on her.

Only her closest people called her "G" and she loved that Kirin had picked up on that.

She'd need that kind of friendship and loyalty to go through what she knew had to be done in Chicago. If she had to sacrifice herself to save Sam, Kirin, and the girl, she would. The leader of the Detroit Mafia could smell an acting job a mile away, so she'd have to commit, but the bigger question is, would Kirin trust her enough to go through with it?

God, she hoped so.

Sam had been in contact with her right up until he went off grid. He'd contacted her man on the inside, found the map and was heading to rescue Arianna, only something had to have gone south.

Kirin wrestled with one of her strappy heels after making it through security, where Gianna could tell every male officer wanted to pat her down. For her part, though, Kirin didn't seem to notice.

When they sat at gate 105D, Kirin got out some gum Gianna had planted in her purse. Her fingers shook as she unwrapped it and popped it in her mouth. Gianna tried not to notice, but in the end couldn't help but ask.

"You afraid to fly?"

"No," Kirin answered, too quickly.

"Then what is it?"

"Nothing."

She was lying. Gianna turned toward her. "Spill."

Kirin glanced up, then looked down at her hands.

"What if he's already gone? They don't seem to wait around when they want someone dead."

Gianna took a deep breath. "My man on the inside says they're after me. They still talk about the double cross and how that's just a death certificate. I think they're dangling Sam out there like a carrot, waiting for me."

Kirin looked at her like she had three heads.

"Did Steve know this?"

Gianna winced. *No. He most certainly did not know this or he wouldn't have agreed to her little plan.*

"Of course," Gianna said and shrugged.

Kirin stared at her a beat, one eyebrow up. "You know, if we're gonna make this work, you have to be honest with me."

Of course…she was right.

Gianna took out a nail file and began filing each nail way too much, like she always did when she didn't want to talk about something.

"What do you want to know?"

Kirin grinned. "Tell me about Steve."

Gianna stopped filing and froze, then resumed without looking at Kirin. "What do you mean? You knew him long before I did." She stated innocently.

Gianna could feel Kirin's stare. She glanced up and found Kirin pinning her with a gaze.

"Fine. I like him. I would never tell him this, but I do. I know his type, though. All American Hero, always does the right thing, always says the right thing. It's too much pressure. I'm not built that way. I screw up, I say the wrong thing…hell, I DO the wrong thing constantly. What could he possibly see in me? I'm just not the right person for him. And he knows it."

Kirin did something that Gianna would've never seen coming if she had all the crystal balls on the planet. She reached out and stopped Gianna's furious fingers from filing her nails down to the nubs. Something Gianna didn't even realize she was doing. She held warm hands on top of Gianna's.

When Gianna looked at her hands then back at Kirin, the kindness in her misty eyes stopped Gianna in her tracks. It made her feel warm and on guard at the same time. Nobody liked her for her. They'd all wanted her for what she could do or give. Always. But this felt different.

Clearing her throat, Kirin said, "G, he loves you. All of you. I think you know that, and I think it scares the shit out of you. But you don't have to know it all right now. Take it slow, enjoy the fact that somebody has your back for once. But listen to me…" Wide eyed, Gianna leaned toward her without even realizing it. "You have to let him inside your circle or you're gonna lose him."

~*~

At that moment, a thin, dark-skinned janitorial worker with a golden front tooth stopped in front of the women deep in conversation, pretending to take care of a full trash can.

What they didn't see was the camera he'd hidden on his cart.

They couldn't possibly have known how much danger they were in.

But he did.

Chapter Fifteen

RD or *Candy* as she'd now be known had to fight for air and to not fall unconscious. Her arms immediately began scratching and yanking at the two massive thighs wrapped around her head.

She was stronger than she looked, but her mind floated in and out of the black. She'd heard herself scream, but the air had been knocked out of her so quickly and her body was pinned, doubled over on herself by the large woman sitting on the back of her neck.

It was a thin line between playing the victim who had been conditioned to do what she was told, to not allowing herself to be put in situations her FBI training couldn't get her out of.

She'd gone through the academy. Grappled against meathead, muscle bound men. She was young, resourceful, and scrappy and yet this overweight, short legged woman had somehow overtaken her at her most vulnerable.

RD's hands were pinching hunks of rippled flesh and pulling with all that she had. She tried pushing up with her legs to rock the woman off her, but leverage was on the large woman's side and RD could feel her body getting weaker and weaker without air.

The corners of her vision were creeping in black, and she knew she had to think of something fast.

Muttering under her breath, the woman grunted and said, "*Hold still you little shit.*"

Tugging down the back right shoulder of RD's top the woman lifted one arm and slammed something hot and metal onto RD's flesh just above her shoulder blade. RD could smell the burning flesh almost before she felt it.

She screamed out in pain as the woman held the metal hot against her skin, hissing like when a plate of fajitas was served hot and steamy at a restaurant. Searing pain mixed with the worst smell invaded RD and for a second she forgot her training. Nausea mixed with her lungs burning, and screaming at her for air, fogged up her brain for a millisecond.

Then it hit her.

She'd been *branded*.

She'd heard that some of the girls came in with messed up scars. Some old and some still scabbing over when they'd been rescued.

Damn it.

She'd been thrown off her game, or she would've put two and two together, the smell and the knowledge. But damnit, trying to remember Mr. Perfect's Face and body had sidetracked her.

All at once, her mind clicked in. She turned her knees to one side, throwing her rider off center. As best she could, she quickly wrapped one ankle around the bottom front leg of the metal chair and used all that she had left to kick the chair out from under them both, all while pushing her body toward the floor to help the chair slip.

The woman on top of her bobbled and tried her hardest to stay on, but her legs were too short.

When the chair finally leaned too far to the left, the woman, RD, the metal branding iron, and the chair came crashing to the floor clanging with such a force, she knew someone would rush in any second.

RD sucked in and gulped air and while her gaze searched for the branding iron. When she spotted it, she dove for it. When she reached it, she jumped up and sprinted to where the large woman struggled to get up.

Raising the hot iron over the evil woman's body, RD was a mere second away from ending this woman's career in branding young, scared women.

She hadn't planned to kill her, just bust up both arms and put her out of service. And maybe her face, just for good measure.

From the floor, the woman had the audacity to laugh, low and throaty.

That's when the door opened.

Sam Neal didn't like risks.

Yeah, he was in the wrong career, and he knew it, but he'd always come out mostly unscathed.

But luck must run out sometime, right?

Pushups in the dark on a cold concrete floor were the only thing keeping his mind and body sharp. Plus, it took the anxiety out of the fact that they'd clamped some damn metal ring around his neck while he was out.

It'd only been a full 24 hours, but Kirin's face in his mind kept reminding him that he needed to find a way out. To come back to her. She deserved not to bury another husband—or husband-to-be in his case.

He shook away the anger he had at himself.

Her last memory would be that they'd argued silently. He'd acted like a baby after she made an offhand comment. But for him, having kids, a wife and a normal life had always been a pipe dream. To be this close to it and not get the entire package, made him feel like a failure.

He knew she didn't mean it. It was just something you said, like, "I'm hungry enough to eat a horse."

His stomach growled on cue.

Wherever he was, they'd put him in a concrete, soundproof room no bigger than a walk-in closet. A small smelly toilet sat in the corner with a mattress on the floor in the other one. It wasn't nearly as nice as a jail cell.

He'd found her. The girl he was supposed to retrieve for Gianna, only she wasn't nearly what G had described. She was *different*.

By now, they'd all know the deal went south. Sam hoped Steve and his team would come, but deep down, he knew that wasn't possible.

Steve had power for sure and he was smitten enough with Gianna, he'd probably do anything she asked, but this was outside Steve's jurisdiction and if he came to help, he'd be fired from the FBI.

That was something even the hope of Gianna's love couldn't convince him to do. It was his entire identity.

The lock on the door rattled as if someone was coming inside. Quickly, Sam scooted from the floor back to the mattress and lay flat as if sleeping. According to his analog watch, which was the only thing they didn't strip him of, it was only five in the morning.

Light cut into the darkness as soon as the door opened. One of Leo's bodyguards stood at the door.

"Up. Now. Time to train."

Sam stood.

This didn't sound good, but he had no choice.

Chapter Sixteen

As they boarded the plane and found their seats in first class, all Kirin could think about was Sam.

They'd argued the night before he disappeared, over the dumbest of things. It was something Kirin had said, halfhearted and off hand, and it'd hurt him.

For that, she was truly sorry.

It started when she'd felt a little nauseous after watching a movie. In truth, it was probably from too much popcorn. She'd grunted when she stood from the couch when the credits rolled. She'd joked out loud that based upon the old lady noises coming out of her, she was too old to have more kids.

Sam had frozen. Stared at her for a beat with a sadness in his eyes that she couldn't unsee.

Seeing this, she'd said quickly, "I'm kidding." Which was like yelling, "time out" as a kid. It meant, it doesn't count. But he didn't see it that way.

Sam had turned, padded into the kitchen and without a word, he'd quietly rinsed out the drink cups, poured the kernels out of the bottom of the popcorn bowls and loaded everything into the dishwasher. It was quiet Sam that broke her heart.

She'd tried to start a few conversations, wanting to tell him that it was just something she'd said off the cuff and didn't mean, but he'd given her one-word answers and busied himself with small chores like taking out the trash and starting a load of laundry.

He was stone cold quiet. For as muscular and strong and pigheaded as he was, deep down, especially when it came to affairs of the heart, he was super inexperienced and soft.

After putting the boys to bed, she went upstairs to find him already showered, light off and rolled away from her side. She sat for a long minute in the dark and silence, listening to his rhythmic breathing and decided not to wake him for what would need to be a long conversation.

By the time she got out of the shower and into bed, he was fully snoring. Her plan to talk to him first thing in the morning didn't pan out either. He'd been long gone by the time she woke.

The only thing he'd left was a ripped piece of paper that said, "Love you. Be safe. ~Sam."

Kirin reached into her purse and rubbed two fingers across the note. It was the only thing she had in her possession that made her feel like herself.

Gianna pulled up the purple velvet eye mask she'd brought to get a quick nap on the plane, shook her head and reached into the purse Kirin was holding. Hoisting it up on her lap, she dug in. When she found the little black box and air pods, she plopped them onto Kirin's lap, chucked the purse in the floor, leaned back while resetting her sleep mask, and said, "Get to work."

Kirin shook her head, feeling the swooped bangs tickle her forehead. She'd almost forgotten that she was completely incognito. Looking at her reflection in the tiny airplane window, she was reminded that she couldn't have looked less like herself if she tried. The absolute only detail that hadn't been permanently changed was her height, but even that was distorted by the giant heels that were currently making her feet throb.

Kirin took a glance down. Great. Her feet were swelling, probably thanks to the dang shoes.

She placed an air pod in each ear, then clicked on the little box. An automated voice told her the air pods were paired.

A small screen lit up with fourteen lessons. Ugh. This was gonna be torture. But Kirin knew the plan and the plan didn't work if anyone recognized her.

She glanced over at Gianna. Boy, she hoped just this once the woman was being honest about all that they needed to do.

But history and some other tickle in the back of her brain, told Kirin she might be wrong.

She just hoped they could get their people and get out.

~*~

When the plane landed in O'Hare, Kirin had dutifully listened to all fourteen modules of speaking and could hear it in her mind. Her inner voice suddenly sounded like she belonged on Jersey Shore.

Gianna woke, pulled off her purple sleep goggles and began dabbing some $100 an ounce crème under her eyes.

Stretching, Gianna shot Kirin a sideways glance.

"What?"

"Did you study or sleep?"

"I studied." Kirin whined in her best Jersey accent.

Gianna's eyebrows rose. She looked both surprised and impressed.

Reaching into her bag, Kirin used the brush and some lipstick. It was time to get into character. Gianna stood and blocked the aisle, letting Kirin out in front.

When the doors opened, Kirin gave a quick nod to Gianna and both women headed up the gangplank. Kirin wasn't exactly sure what to expect, but Gianna had let her in on a few details.

They were to grab an Uber and head to a tourist attraction in Niles, a town about twenty-five minutes from the airport.

There, they'd take some pictures around the Leaning Tower of Niles (meant to replicate the Leaning Tower of Pisa) and that would be the signal to meet their contact around the backside.

From that point, the plan got a little hazier, but she still understood the main points. Gianna, for her part, had gotten quiet.

They stepped on to the long escalator with Gianna one step down from Kirin. At the bottom was a flurry of people walking toward the long line of rental car stands and milling around luggage corrals waiting for the red light to spin indicating that their bags would be dropping on to the conveyor belt.

Kirin sucked in a breath when she spotted him.

Muscled up like a professional wrestler, a man with tattoos from his wrist to his neck stood in a wide stance close to the bottom of the escalator. He wore a scowl and had G's bag sitting at his feet, but not Kirin's.

In his hands, he held a sign that read "Gianna Calamia."

Kirin elbowed Gianna and stared at the man. G followed her line of sight then cursed under her breath.

Kirin could read the panic on Gianna's face like a map. This wasn't supposed to happen. The man had her bag. Her bag had the damn gun. Without the gun, she was powerless against these people. Gianna stood for a beat working it out. Then, like a flash of lightning, Gianna turned her back toward the bottom, facing only Kirin. Her eyes open wide and wild.

She reached into her purse and pulled out a small, purple Crown Royal bag fit for an airplane bottle. She shoved it inside Kirin's purse.

"Quick, put that in the inside pocket. The one with a zipper."

Kirin did as she was asked. "What is it?"

"Don't lose that. Understand? Not only is it my favorite, but it has something very valuable in it. You're on your own." She took a quick glance back at the man, then stared at Kirin for a beat as if deciding what to tell her.

"Hyde Park. Penthouse inside the Sophy. First, go to Niles, find our contact. Guard this purse with your life. Do you understand?"

Kirin nodded.

Then as quickly as she'd spoken, she turned on her heel, pulled on her sunglasses and stepped down a few steps as if she and Kirin were strangers. When she reached the bottom, Gianna raised one arm gently and smiled at the gruff looking man.

He looked her up and down, lowered the sign, picked up her bag and led her outside by the arm. From an outsider's point of view, it probably appeared as if he was just escorting her, but Kirin knew he was taking her.

G, for her part, raised her chin and walked elegantly.

She never looked back.

And Kirin was on her own.

Chapter Seventeen

Electricity ran through RD in a hot second. The clicking sound of a taser attached to her torso rang in her ears.

Lucky for her, she'd been trained through this one, and no over-the-counter civilian taser was as strong as the one used on her in training.

She had but three seconds before her body would fall to the floor in convulsions, but luckily, her swings were quick and accurate.

The woman yelled out in pain as the metal bar found purchase first in one arm, then on the backswing, the second arm.

RD had the good sense to drop the iron off to the side as her body seized and she fell to the ground. Thank God the training had included the correct way to fall, or she'd have cracked her dome on the concrete floor.

People rushed into the room and flicked on the light. RD stayed alert, as she'd been trained, reading lips of the people in the room when the ringing in her ears hadn't subsided yet. Her heart rate increased immediately, but she reminded herself it was temporary.

The large man with the scowl held the taser as two other men ran into the room and helped the woman up. They had to talk about it for several seconds as they couldn't lift her and couldn't use her arms to help her stand. Finally, they devised a plan and got her to her feet.

She glared at RD then stomped toward her stiff body, reared back her giant thigh and foot, poised to kick RD in the face.

All RD could do was close her eyes. The feeling hadn't yet returned fully in her arms.

Just as her hearing was beginning to return, she heard a man yell what sounded like one Chinese word and the entire room stopped.

The electricity from the taser had been halted, the large woman took a step away and instantly switched her angry gaze from RD's face to the young man standing at the door.

RD followed her line of sight. The man stared at her a beat, his face held stern anger, jaw tight and lips straight and taut. Somehow, he looked younger today in jeans, a T-shirt and a ballcap, but his eyes held a mixture of anger, sadness, and something else she couldn't place. She wondered if she was the only one who could see it.

He made one motion, and the two men ran to RD, lifted her, and straightened her appearance.

Her shoulder blade felt like it had a knife sticking out of it and her body was weak and sore, but on the plus side, she hadn't soiled herself due to the wattage running through her body as some do, and she was alive. Had the woman kicked her, she'd have a pretty messed up face by now, too.

The two men walked RD toward the man at the door. The large man who'd stood in the corner, still holding the yellow taser stared from RD to the young man as if he knew something.

Both men froze, locked in a look that somehow spoke volumes. RD tried to keep her gaze low and stay in character, but the relationship between these two made the air crackle and was obviously tumultuous.

The young leader nodded to those inside, speaking something in Chinese she didn't understand, then he turned, holding on to RD's left arm, leading her down along the hallway, through two sets of double doors, down two flights of stairs and into a private, locked garage tucked at the back of a public parking lot.

He hadn't looked her way or even spoken, just walked briskly as if they had a plane to catch. Which, if her intel was correct, they probably did.

When he opened her car door, placed her inside, buckled her seatbelt, and reached over her to hit the button for the garage door to open, it felt like a weird date in a dream. He smelled of rich leather and a clean smelling soap. Somewhere deep inside, he must've known she wouldn't run, as he made no attempt to lock her inside the vehicle, or cuff her or anything.

When he sat, she took a deep breath trying to decide what to say as he fastened his seatbelt and started the car. He obviously knew who she was, that had been established. So, what was the harm in breaking character? He was obviously still taking her somewhere to get his money.

Plus, she'd put a few fuzzy memories together that morning. And if he was who she thought he was, she knew how to get him to talk.

As was her custom, jump first and then figure out how to land, RD wrestled for a grand total of three seconds before she decided.

"So," she began, as he pulled out of the garage, closed it and headed for the exit, "tell me, *Bo*, how do you get from junior partner in one of Knoxville's biggest law firms to a life of crime? Seems like a big stretch in character, right?"

His jaw tightened. He stared straight ahead, twisting, and turning around alleys to get out of downtown for so long that she didn't think he planned to respond.

Oh, her memory had come back. With vengeance.

After a long couple of moments, Bo spoke.

But when he did, she immediately wished she hadn't shown her cards.

Chapter Eighteen

Chicago

Kirin had never been to Chicago. Had she not been born with the disability of zero sense of direction, she might have thought it exciting. Her mind swirled and she shuffled from one foot to the other, waiting for her luggage and trying to remember every nugget of information just in case she'd missed something.

The plan—well, at least the plan she'd been told—was that they were going to dangle something in front of Leo, the head of the Detroit Mafia to bargain for the lives of Sam and Gianna's adopted daughter's sister.

But what? G never told her the entire plan. Only bits and pieces. What if they took Gianna to a different location? She'd never find her. She'd not made Kirin privy to all the details and now, she was gone.

When the red light finally came on, Kirin's was one of the first off the plane. She found the lime green ribbon she'd tied to her black rolling bag, hoisted it up, pulled the handle and pulled it over to the side. She needed a minute.

She found a bench off to the side from the hustle and bustle of the luggage return and sat. She opened her wallet and found cash and a credit card with her new name on it. Thank God.

Kirin knew the underworld. She'd listened in on enough of Steve, and Sam's conversations to know that ears were always listening, and eyes were always on, especially if you were the hunted. She glanced around. Either she was becoming a bit paranoid, or the few people who stood near her were staring at her.

It was the outfit, she decided. They were probably wondering when she'd start her shift on the corner.

She'd need to be on her toes. It would take her new voice, new look and everything she had not to fall into the same traps. Digging back into her purse she found her makeup bag and mirror. Channeling a little bit of G's arrogance, Kirin pulled out the mirror and snapped it open. She tried to remember not to gasp when she saw her appearance. Applying lipstick and a little eyeliner, she smoothed down her hair, snapped it closed and tossed it all back inside.

After pulling out cash for a cab, Kirin zipped up the purse, then slipped the straps down the handle of her rolling luggage.

As she stood, her stomach did a queasy dance, she breathed through it, remembering she hadn't had anything to eat in several hours.

Walking out into the sunlight, the line of cabs darting in and out of the fire lane seemed like bees around a hive. It was both intimidating and impressive.

Throngs of people stood in lines to catch one. The chilly air was very different than Spring in Knoxville. It felt more like Winter and Kirin cursed the low-cut shirt she'd been made to wear. She hunched over slightly as she tried to find the shortest cab line amidst all the noise and people.

She followed like cattle to the shortest line waiting for a cab. When it was her turn, the fast talking, heavy-set man hailing cabs stuck out his hand. Kirin pressed a five-dollar bill in it, hoping it was enough. The man didn't even look at the money, just shoved it inside a zipper pouch attached at his hip and started yelling at the cab driver who'd just pulled up.

Apparently, drivers needed to pull within inches of the curb and this one hadn't. Plus, as soon as he put the cab in park, he opened his door and stood, staring over the top of the cab, scanning the crowd. He had jacked-up, obviously colored jet-black hair and wore an eye patch. Something in his voice, even yelling and with a thick accent tickled the back of Kirin's brain as if she'd heard it before but couldn't place it.

This act of standing outside your cab was apparently much like treason.

The man hailing cabs began screaming at him and everyone in line craned their necks to see the drama. Eye patch man yelled back that he was supposed to pick someone specific up and the two argued that he was in the wrong place for that.

When the cabbie refused to move and refused to open his trunk for Kirin's bag, the man next to her opened the back door of the cab, tossed her bag inside, landing perfectly on the seat behind the driver, then gently shoved Kirin inside.

Eye patch screamed out at the man and gave his favorite finger after many choice words. He slammed his door and burnt his tires getting away.

Kirin tried to put her seatbelt on, since anger and driving didn't seem to mix for this guy. She grabbed the seatback when he turned the car so sharply, she could've sworn they were on two wheels. The cab missed tagging another car's side mirror by inches.

Finally, remembering her trained speech, she yelled,

"Hey! You got a person back here."

The man glared at her for a beat in the rearview mirror then declared, "I'm literally dropping you at the next corner, lady. I'm late to pick my passenger up. I'll give you the number of the cab company. Somebody else will take you the rest of the way.

Sweat pooled around his hairline. His accent had been so thick that it took her several seconds for her brain to catch exactly what he was saying.

Kirin channeled her inner, angry, southern woman, but kept her Jersey accent.

"No! You *will* take me to The Leaning Tower of Niles. I'm meeting someone and I'm late. You got plenty of time for that.

The man scooted over two lanes at the next light and squealed to a stop at a gas station. He shut off the cab and turned his entire body toward her, sneering.

"Get out." He commanded.

It was then she saw it.

The one thing that told her exactly who this man was.

Chapter Nineteen

Knoxville, TN

Bo Huang could have spit nails.

It'd taken him all of ten seconds to realize he knew the girl who stood before him. Just his freaking luck.

He'd never asked for this damn double life. That'd been his asshat uncle's doing.

When Bo's uncle died, Bo's father charged him with helping to run his younger brother's exporting business. Only the elder brother didn't understand exactly what his black sheep younger brother had been exporting.

In Bo's culture, the eldest brother took over as parent when the parents passed away. This meant that his cousin Al, also known as the biggest screw-up in the family (other than his father's younger brother) was now second in command—to Bo.

And Al hated him for it.

The idiot should've rightfully inherited his father's stupid business, but he was now governed by Bo's father.

Bo absolutely didn't want this life, but when your father asked you to do something, you did it, without question.

That was his first mistake.

By the time Bo got ahold of his uncle's spreadsheets and figured out exactly what they were doing, he was already in too deep to go back to his normal life.

And the worst part was, he couldn't tell his father the truth.

But now that *he* knew, he had to find a way to stop it. But to do this, he'd have to play the game.

He'd been toiling non-stop trying to find a solution that simultaneously shut this underworld down, didn't ruin his future career in law, and didn't upset his aging father.

Bo scrubbed his face.

Before this week, he'd never processed a human before. He damn sure had never processed a girl he *knew* either.

He cut his eyes toward her.

All this time, he'd thought all that drunken FBI talk was made up. At the bar that night, she'd come on to him in the most bizarre way, basically telling him that even though she wore a nun costume, she was trained and could kick his ass, with five other guys looking on.

She was a tiny powerhouse with curves and a backside that made a bad decision after a hellish day in court look like a walk in the park. He'd fallen hard. She'd left, changed her number, and ghosted him.

He'd even seen her once downtown after that night, but as soon as he'd gotten a good look, she'd vanished.

Now, she sat next to him, beat to shit, bleeding from her shoulder and still, she baited him.

At the next redlight, he looked straight ahead and answered her, "Selling yourself into this world shouldn't be a stretch for someone like you. This is probably just a game to you so that you'll get used. Trust me when I say, being *used* feels pretty shitty."

She had the common decency to look down at her hands, then out the window. When she finally spoke, her voice cracked.

"It does." Then she turned back toward him. But, why? Why would you sell young girls to monsters that will use them? Other than money to pay for your stupid suits and your stupid car, which I'm sure your law salary already pays for, what could possibly make this okay for you?"

Bo wanted to tell her that he'd been forced into helping. That at first, he'd only stepped in a couple of nights a week. It didn't take long for them to push him into the driver's seat. He'd taken it, because that's what you do when someone you love asks for help, you help them.

After all, he was the eldest son, and this was how it was done in their culture.

But his father had made a promise that protected Bo's Uncle. He'd promised that Bo would keep his business going. Somehow promises don't die when awful men do. And now, Bo's dreams of becoming a full-fledged partner in his law firm were dead.

Finally, he answered her. "This isn't my business. I'm filling in for someone else."

RD stared at him like he had horns sticking out.

"So, you're saying that since you are just a temporary worker, that it's all okay? That you have zero moral code to do the right thing?"

When he didn't answer, she shook her head, her gaze boring into his soul. "Man, taken as a whole, I gave you far too much credit. I mistook you for one of the good guys."

"You wouldn't understand," Bo spat.

RD looked straight out the windshield in disgust, as if looking at him was turning her stomach, "I understand right and wrong. You obviously don't. Which makes the fact that you're in *law*, even worse. I guess that Halloween costume was real."

Bo could feel the heat rising in his cheeks. When he spoke, it was just below a yell, "Can we suffice it to say that I'm doing this against my will? I'm fully aware of how wrong it is and I'm trying to make it right. But right now, I'm stuck. And I must take the only girl who has sparked my interest since college, to the worst place on the planet. So, how about we just shut up and deal with what we have?"

RD turned slowly, "Your serious right now? *You* never called. Don't be pulling the *"you're the girl for me,"* crap when you had my number and didn't use it."

Bo sped up to beat a semi on the interstate as he was merging toward the airport. To be honest, his foot would've hit the floor anyway. He cracked a window to get some air. Once merged, he glanced over at her and lowered his voice to a growl.

"You gave me a fake number that was disconnected from the first time I dialed it, to the last."

RD opened her mouth then shut it. He watched her every few seconds. She stared, red faced and wide eyed, out the windshield for several minutes, then bit her lip.

"I did that." She whispered.

He turned and met her eye to eye. The remorse was real regardless of if she was a good actress.

She took a breath and continued, speaking more to herself than him. "I used do it without thinking. I sabotaged myself assuming that nobody wants a girlfriend who could be sent on a mission at two am with the very high possibility that she won't return. I honestly thought I'd broken that bad habit and had given you the right number. And here, I've blamed you the whole time. Thought you just wanted me for one night."

Bo's heart dropped in his stomach.

They drove for several minutes in silence.

When he passed the airport and kept driving, she glanced over at him.

"You missed the exit."

"I know."

RD turned and looked back at the airport over her shoulder, then back at him.

"You have to turn around." Her voice sounded panicked.

"No, I don't."

"Yes, you do." She said louder as if he hadn't heard the first time.

RD placed her hand on his arm and their eyes locked. Hers pleading. Bo turned onto a road he'd never been on before and found an empty church parking lot. When he parked and turned off the car, he stared straight ahead.

"You know I can't do this now."

"Look at me," she commanded.

Bo took a deep breath and turned toward her. Dark eyes that had been once lit with laughter, mostly at him, now pierced him.

"You must take me to the airport. I've prepared myself, I've trained for this, and I have someone on the inside waiting for me. Hell. I've been *branded* today. I've got to move down the line in order to stop this."

He winced at that. But she shook her head and continued.

"This is my journey. I chose this and I have to go through with it. I don't blame you one bit." At this she reached out and touched his arm. "It sounds like someone has a hold on you making you do this. But right now, is not the time to wake up your conscience.

Right now, I need you to hand me over so I can complete my mission."

As her words were sinking in, Bo's phone rang.

"Yeah?"

"Why you not at airport?" His slimy cousin said in broken English.

"Heading there now. Had to stop and…control."

"Good. Get there."

Bo stared at RD for a beat. She flashed a smile meant to comfort him that twisted his gut even more.

RD reached over and turned the engine back on and rubbed her hands as if she were excitedly waiting for a ride at Dollywood. Then she smiled, reassuringly.

"This is dangerous and stupid; you know that right?" Bo said as he backed out of the parking space and headed for the airport.

"Yep," RD said with a smile. "And it's gonna work."

He feared she was dead wrong.

Chapter Twenty

Chicago, IL

"That has got to be the worst disguise I've ever seen. And my God, your accent is terrible. Where did you get it?" Kirin asked, giggling.

The man's face turned purple.

"I said, get out." He yelled louder and through gritted teeth.

"Nope. Why are you here? Does Sam know you're here?"

The moment she mentioned Sam's name, the man's eyebrows pushed together and then released in a split second.

His accent was even thicker now. "I don't know who you think I am lady, but I want you out of my cab, right now."

Quicker than she thought possible, the man opened his door, ran around the back of the car, and flung open hers. Kirin crossed her arms. She wasn't moving an inch to take the seatbelt off.

And seriously? She didn't look that different, did she?

When he came at her with both hands to angrily pull her seatbelt off and her body out, she realized her mistake.

Using her *real* voice, she said, "Seth...shoot, Joel...whatever...It's me. It's Kirin. Stop!"

The man froze for a beat, studying her face. Then leaned over, ignored her words, and started ripping at her seatbelt again as if he hadn't heard her.

"I swear to God, I'm gonna kick you in the face like I did the day you kidnapped me. Remember...I sewed up your neck in the backseat? I can see your scar. If I wasn't me, how would I know about that??"

Joel froze for a beat, then slowly sat back on his heels, and stared at her.

"Let's see, what can I tell you that will convince you, it's really me..."

She smiled when it hit her, "I know! You told me that Kidd hired you, before you told your brother, Sam. And I got to be the one to break it to him in my living room after Thanksgiving dinner this past year."

Joel's shoulders fell about an inch. He stared for another few seconds, shook his head then gently shut her door. He walked back around the front talking to himself and climbed inside.

Before he started the car, he turned back around to stare at her.

Kirin held one hand up, with eyebrows raised. "I know, I know. Gianna's work. This..." she pointed at herself up and down, "took four hours and three people."

Joel shook his head, turned back toward the steering wheel and chuckled.

"The name is Katy," Kirin said, shaking her head.

"Damn. I don't think even Sam would recognize you." Joel said as he pulled out in traffic.

"That's the plan." She mumbled more to herself than him.

Chapter Twenty-One

Chicago

Gianna wasn't taken to the right place.

Not even close.

Instead of the penthouse at the Sophy, she was driven inside the massive open bay doors of a dungy warehouse.

One that looked like from the inside it was crumbling around its ears. The outside hadn't looked nearly as bad.

When the ogre who'd picked her up at the airport grabbed her bag and walked around and opened her door, the smell of jet fuel swirled in her nostrils.

She stood and adjusted her purse on her shoulder as if she'd been about to walk the red carpet.

You never knew who was watching.

Just outside the bay doors was a private jet, flashy yet elegant. Just her style.

The bodyguard motioned for her to follow as he led the way on to the tarmac toward the stairs. Without a word he pointed to the top of the stairs as he stowed her rolling bag below.

Gianna took a deep breath, chin high and started up the metal staircase.

Loud music invaded her ears. The thumping of the bass caused the stairs to shimmy a little as she began her ascent, but it'd been turned down by the time she got to the top. When she reached it, there was no pilot or anyone to greet her, she turned to see one well-dressed man, eyebrows furrowed, frowning at his phone. He sat in a white leather swivel chair at a small marble table with two flutes of champagne sitting in front of him.

The inside of the cabin smelled fresh and leathery and was well appointed and luxurious.

The stunning man glanced up at her, stashed his phone and smiled the most brilliant white smile that matched his shirt. Then he took and raised his glass, motioning for her to sit across from him.

The dark-skinned man looked as if he just fell out of a Gucci ad. Dark eyes watched her every curve appreciatively, while his jaw, even while smiling, did that sexy thing where the muscles engage. She almost couldn't look away, like she was caught in a snare. He was damn near beautiful, sitting open legged with manly attitude, like a cross between Tyrese and Tupac.

Gianna smiled, swung her hips, lowered her purse, and sat gingerly crossing her ankles.

"Now this, is how I expect a meeting to start." Gianna lifted her glass to his, clinked it and pretended to drink. She was no dummy.

As beautiful as this man was, right now, she was being taken against her will. She just might need to keep saying that over and over in her head. Normally, it was her that had the upper hand on wowing people when they walked in somewhere.

She didn't like the taste of her own medicine.

After he finished his sip, never taking his eyes off her, he spoke. "Welcome. I hope you had a nice trip?"

Gianna nodded and got right to the point. "Who are you?"

"You're correct. I'm sorry. Introduction first. My name is D'Angelo. Yours?"

Gianna shifted herself in her seat. It was the only way to mask her hands that immediately trembled.

"Gianna. Nice to meet you."

He eyed her curiously. "You've heard of me?"

Gianna shrugged, then pulled her glass up to her lips, parted them but didn't drink. Hell yeah, she'd heard of him. The leader of the entire eastern seaboard of trafficking. Basically, Leo's boss, although Leo would never admit it. She wondered when she'd meet this guy. All of a sudden her plan had a twist she didn't see coming. Her mind chased down all possible endings. Maybe, just maybe she could use this.

When she didn't answer, he smiled. "I've heard of you." He said casually.

Gianna lowered the glass and set it back on the spotless marble table. She uncrossed her ankles and leaned forward.

"From Leo?"

The man nodded, then added, "Let's just say he's going to be unhappy when he finds out I have you, instead of him."

Gianna watched him for a beat. Then decided to try an experiment; play dumb.

"So, you're not friends?" She leaned back and asked as innocently as she could.

His eyes danced although his face didn't change.

"Not exactly."

Gianna nodded and then smiled.

D'Angelo leaned forward, looking intrigued. "What is it?" he asked.

"Let's cut to the chase. You have something I want, and I have something you want. Are we to make a deal or not?"

D'Angelo sat back in his chair, fingers steepled. He watched her for a few moments, then answered.

"I think what I have, is more valuable to you than what you have for me."

"I doubt it." She quipped, then waited for him to finish.

"I have a new deal for you. One that you really can't refuse."

The pilot shut the door and it took everything Gianna had not to jump at the sound. She stared back at D'Angelo until the flight attendant came and replaced their drinks with cold bottled waters and asked that they both fasten their seatbelts.

D'Angelo stashed his water bottle in the built in cup on his seat, then stood.

"Excuse me. I'll be right back." He flashed her a quick smile, then headed for the cockpit that was visible from where she sat.

Gianna quickly fastened her seatbelt, opened her water, specifically making sure she could feel the three clicks indicating it had been a fresh, unopened bottle, then she chugged some. She placed it in her built-in cup on her chair just as he had.

She turned the swivel chair slightly so that she could see them both and strained attempting to hear the conversation, but the engines were revved, and the plane was turning. As soon as he'd spoken, the pilot reached over and said something into his radio.

D'Angelo said a few more words, chuckled at something the pilot said, then made his way back toward the table. He moved like a strong lion, sexy and confident, pinning her with his eyes at every step.

Lord, she'd met her match with this one.

Chapter Twenty-Two

Knoxville

When Bo pulled into the parking lot, he shut off the car, popped the trunk and got out. RD knew the drill. Cameras were everywhere and she needed to appear as if she was demure and moved with him on command.

Bo wrestled around with something in the trunk for a few seconds and then emerged with two backpacks slung on his back. This was the most precarious part of the trip. Bo would have to get them through security and on to the plane without anyone raising eyebrows. With Homeland Security scouring each flight looking for trafficked young women, they'd both need to be on point with their acting skills.

Some of her research indicated that the kidnappers would make the young girls pretend they were a niece, daughter or girlfriend depending on their age. Since she and Bo were super close in age, it'd have to be girlfriend.

When he opened her door, his jaw was tight. Holding out a hand, she took it as he helped her out of the car. Damn if her shoulder blade wasn't on fire. She was glad she'd decided to wear black as the wound had to be bleeding. She dreaded putting that backpack on. She reached out her other hand to grab it from him, but he shook his head and carried both packs.

Still holding her hand, they strolled through the covered parking garage as a cool breeze slid past them. RD tried to pretend that they were a couple going on vacation. Her hand fit perfectly in his. His hands weren't rough like the men she worked with; they were smooth. For a split second, her mind drifted back to spotty memories of that night. Until she shut them down.

Yep. Smooth hands.

She had to shake her head to get those visions out.

Bo glanced down at her with a question in his eyes and a slight smile on his lips as though he could see into her mind.

God, she hoped not.

When they passed through the automatic sliding doors, Bo headed for the counter to buy the tickets, holding tight to her hand. If he'd let her go, that would raise a red flag to those she knew were stationed there to watch him and ensure he was putting her on the plane like he should.

When it was their turn, he paid for the tickets, held them in his other hand and led her up the slick corridor toward Security. As they stood in line, he dropped her hand for a beat, set both backpacks on the floor and asked for her ID.

As she pulled it out of the pack, she thought of the best game.

"Name one thing you know about me."

"What?" He looked at her like she was crazy.

"Trying to make this fun."

He shot her a side glance like she was crazy as they moved up in line.

"Come on, please? It'll make us less nervous. You can only answer True, False, yes or no."

Bo took a step forward, with his back toward her, then turned, whispering back to her. "Your FBI idiots didn't call you by your real name."

"True." She lifted on tip toes and whispered, grinning happily, that he was playing along. "Now, your turn."

Bo thought for a beat, then turned toward her, "You would've said yes to a second, and much better date, than the first one."

Something hit in the pit of her stomach. Yes. Most definitely yes, she would've. But she knew herself. She would've been guarded and probably screwed it up.

"Ah…" she hesitated, watching his eyes narrow.

"You have to tell the truth." He warned.

RD rolled her eyes, "Fine…true."

He grinned, smug. When it was their turn to walk to the podium staffed by two Homeland Security Officers who'd been watching them, they checked their ID's and passed them through without any hesitation.

When they were out of earshot and heading toward the conveyor belt station, RD stepped in front of him and whispered, "Told ya."

Suddenly, Bo seemed super nervous. His gaze darted from one guard to the next at each of the four lines. Just as they were lined up in one fast paced line and she was about to take her shoes off, Bo pulled her bad arm toward the far lane.

Once they were in that line, Bo glanced back and frowned. Her face must've betrayed her and briefly registered pain. He leaned down, inches from her face, waited for her to glance up at him then whispered, "I'm sorry. I forgot."

RD felt the tug. The pull of having someone show compassion and the sincerity of his voice. Usually, emotions like this made her shrink back, but not this time. She took them in, shrugged, then began taking her shoes off.

Bo stared for another beat before switching his gaze to the short security guard who watched his monitor as if he was protecting the President.

RD would bet that one of their backpacks had a weapon in it. Hell, if she could've gotten away with her gun, she would've.

The man finally felt Bo's gaze and glanced up. For a brief second, they stared at one another like two gunslingers in the middle of a dusty town. The shorter man's unflinching face indicated he'd not be helpful today.

Bo nodded at him. The man froze, then quickly regained his composure. She watched for a signal. She'd been told they used an elaborate dictionary of signals that the everyday person wouldn't even notice. The man picked up his coffee cup from the right side of his keyboard, took a sip and placed it on the left, then glanced back at his screen. A few seconds later, he nodded. It was so quick, only the truly observant would've caught it and she did.

It fully amazed her how intricate this web of deceit ran. People all over were in on a piece of the billion-dollar industry that generally was visible just under the regular world's nose, only most people were so caught up in their own lives, they rarely took the time to see it.

All at once, she was both grateful for the slide and pissed.

Somehow when Bo went through the security scan he passed with flying colors, but when RD went through it, alarms beeped as if she were trying to steal the Mona Lisa.

The man behind the counter motioned toward the second officer to take her aside and scan her with the wand. Out of the corner of her eye, while standing spread eagle and being frisked and scanned, she saw the short man's nimble quick fingers typing something into his keyboard.

When they finished examining her and let her go, Bo was smiling as if he had something up his sleeve.

"Are you serious? Why did they scan me and not you?"

Bo gathered up his things and shrugged, not so innocently.

"Maybe you look more like a criminal than I do." He answered, dimples pinching in on his cheeks.

"Doubt it," she said, pulling her shoes back on.

Bo considered her statement and nodded. When they both had their things, he intertwined his fingers in with hers. This wasn't just grabbing her hand for show. This felt personal, intimate. Part of her—albeit a small part— didn't mind at all. The rest of her needed desperately to focus on the problem at hand.

While walking toward their gate, Bo veered off to the right and led her into the airport store. Inside he bought Band-Aids, Neosporin, Ibuprofen, and a small travel pack of wet wipes, thanked the cashier and led RD out toward the only restaurant and bar in that wing at McGee Tyson.

Seated in a high sided booth toward the back, Bo insisted that she sit on the inside and on the same side as him, facing away from the rest of the eyes in the bar.

Ordering burgers and beers for both as soon as the waitress dropped off waters, Bo waited a beat for her to leave, then got right to work.

"Quick, take your shirt off." He said, completely serious.

"Uh, no. good try though. I'm not that easy."

Eyebrows up, he shot her a look.

"Ha. You knew what I meant."

"It'll get infected if I don't clean it," Bo said as he forced open the Ibuprofen bottle and shook two out. He placed them in front of her and made a motion for her to turn.

RD exhaled, then winced again as she reluctantly turned her chest toward the wall and pulled the back of her shirt up and over her bloody shoulder. No need to take the shirt off, thank you.

Quickly and carefully, he cleaned the wound, spread Neosporin over the fresh scab and bandaged it.

No sooner had she pulled her shirt down than the waitress delivered their beers.

The condescending look she shot them indicated she was sure they were doing something wrong. When she flitted away, RD said, "My turn."

Bo took a long pull of his beer and watched her out of the corner of his eye. An understanding passed between them until he finally announced, "Shoot."

RD asked the one question she wasn't sure she wanted the answer to.

"What does my new tattoo say?"

When Bo's face turned white, she knew it couldn't be good.

Chapter Twenty-Three

Kirin watched store after store zoom by as Joel drove her toward the Leaning Tower of Niles, a touristy locale that did not resemble its namesake in size, but according to the sign, it did light up at night.

The fifteen-minute drive from O'Hare was mostly quiet. Joel spoke a little about his family, but never a word about their current mission. The unspoken subject of him dropping her off to be met by a stranger didn't seem to ever scratch the surface, but it was obviously the elephant in the cab.

Yes, she knew it was a long shot and yes, she knew it was dangerous, but whatever it took to get Sam back, she'd gladly do. He'd put his life on the line for hers so many times and her life didn't make sense without him.

But she'd been fighting the mob for so long, and she was so ready to be done with all the missions and the undercover work. She wondered what would help him to see that she and the boys needed him, all of him, more than he needed the rush.

Joel slowed when he got to the parking lot of the attraction. His gaze darted from the road to his rearview mirror and back several times.

Finally, Kirin spoke, "It's okay, you know."

"What?"

"That you drop me and leave."

Joel stared at her for a beat, then switched his gaze back to finding a spot to park. When he found one, he parked and turned toward the back seat.

"Why don't you let me go instead?"

"No. The only way this works is if they don't recognize me. They'd remember you; you stood behind me in the living room where they watched Todd and Nicky die. They saw your face. You can't get past them, like I can."

Joel shook his head. "I feel like my brother is going to kick my ass for not stopping you from getting out of this car."

"I'm not gonna tell him I knew the one eyed cab driver." Kirin smiled. Joel returned it halfheartedly. "I do need a favor though?"

Joel nodded, "Anything."

"I need for you *not* to get out of the car."

As she said it, she stuck her hand forward to him so that anyone outside the car would think she was handing him cash to pay her bill. Joel held on to her hand for a few seconds too long, searching her eyes.

"You sure about this?" he asked as he let go.

"Yep. Now pop the trunk."

~*~

Chicago's weather was just as bipolar as Knoxville. Crazy windy with a frosty draft one minute and the next, no breeze with the sun beating down on the back of your neck.

Kirin pulled her rolling bag behind her and walked the circumference of the Leaning Tower of Niles, to no avail. Nobody touched her on the arm and gave her the stupid password. Nobody even stood behind her commenting like Kidd had done when she met him at a Braves game. People milled around, taking pictures as if they were holding the statue up on the palm of their hand, or taking selfies with it, while others seemed to be reading pamphlets about its history or chasing toddlers.

One kid with long blonde hair covering one eye, ran through on a skateboard in front of her about a hundred times. Finally, she found a bench facing the structure and sat down. Damn if she wasn't just tired.

And she knew exactly why.

With a tight grip on her purse attached to her rolling bag with a carabiner, she closed her eyes and told herself it was just for a second.

108

A thin shadow covered her. Alarms sounded from somewhere in her sleepy mind. With a jolt, Kirin sat upright and wide eyed, as if someone was there to steal her bag, or worse. She squinted and shielded her eyes.

When they focused, a thin black man in a grey beanie hat stood before her. When the hot sun caught and glimmered off his one gold tooth, he immediately recited the one word she'd been waiting to hear, "Terhune?"

Kirin gazed at his worn face. He looked to be in his sixties. His smile was kind, but his eyes were shifty. This made her hyperaware as she automatically mimicked him and began glancing around.

Kirin cleared her throat, stuck out her hand and put on her best accent, reciting the word she was supposed to, "Sonny."

Immediately the man's shoulders lowered, but his gaze still shifted behind her.

"Where is the other woman?"

"Someone took her at the airport."

The man swore under his breath, then exhaled loudly. "Well, that changes things a bit."

He stared at her for a beat, clearly thinking, then asked, "Did you have a cab?"

"I did, but it's gone."

"We need to move." he said, reaching for her bag.

Kirin shook her head, and he froze.

"I need your name, first."

"David. David Ardo."

"Nice to meet you."

Chapter Twenty-Four

Literally, he had no words.

Couldn't have formed them even if he knew what he wanted to say.

Sam couldn't feel his limbs, nor did he want to. Those third world evil people had scrambled his brain. He tried to concentrate, stating his name over and over in his mind as if he was afraid if he didn't, he'd forget it. But where did he live? What was his job? Everything was so jumbled up. Sitting on the cold floor of the blacked-out room, he gently pressed his palms into his sore eye sockets praying it would cease the pounding in his brain.

Yeah, he'd been pummeled repeatedly and knocked unconscious, but while he was out, they must've bound his hands with rope since he had burns on both wrists. His hair was matted with sweat and tight sores lined his scalp that felt like they'd poked needles into his brain. He knew what that had been.

He'd woken once, electrodes attached to his scalp that shot through who-knew how many kilowatts of electricity. Oh, and thanks to a bandage on his arm, they must've injected something into his bloodstream, too. God only knew what that would do to him.

And of course, the damn metal collar was still in place sending random electricity and causing one hell of a headache. But this was no ordinary headache. It hurt like a migraine, but it was so much more than just pain. It was as if somehow the collar interfered with his memory. Hell, even just tying his shoes took serious effort when it hummed. Or remembering his own name.

All of it, just shy of killing him, he knew that much.

His nose had bled profusely and when they'd finished, he'd thrown up everything he had in his stomach and had passed back out.

When he woke, the world was different. Black, confused and he was back in his original darkened room as if he'd dreamed the whole thing.

Voices rang outside his door. He held his breath. Surely, they weren't coming for round two. Sam strained to hear. Spanish. Did he know Spanish? He pushed his brain even further to listen for words he might understand.

Nope. Not a word.

For a beat he stared at his hands letting his eyes adjust to the darkness. No ring. Why did he think he was married? Was he supposed to be married by now?

Then it hit him.

Kirin. The boys. Knoxville. His life.

But it seemed distant, like a mountain off in the expanse that you can see but know you'll never be able to climb.

And without his tracking device he knew they'd never find him. But this mind-bending torture would eventually change him, of that, he was sure.

He'd need a solid plan before they came back to get him. Sam struggled to envision the young woman they'd whisked away. Sam realized much too late that she'd been the bait. He thought she'd have been scared and was willing to escape with him.

But in her he found a tumultuous attitude and stubbornness for which he was completely unprepared.

Chapter Twenty-Five

Gianna held her own in light conversation for the moments it took to taxi on the runway and take off. When the aircraft banked left and began to head South instead of North, where she assumed they'd take her, her eyebrows furrowed.

He noticed.

"A change in plans," he answered lightly as if reading her mind.

"Where?"

"My vacation home."

Gianna's mind raced. Kirin was in Chicago, where she'd sent Sam to find Arianna. Now she was headed to God only knew where, which meant...getting her daughter back was now in the hands of Kirin.

She prayed Kirin had found the contact, that he was legit and that she'd find the things she needed to get everyone home safe and go through with the plan.

D'Angelo watched her curiously, then spoke.

"What are you willing to exchange for the man you sent to Chicago to steal one of my girls?"

Gianna swallowed hard. Here's where she'd see just how important or unimportant the information she'd bought would be.

"Intel."

Smooth and unaffected, his eyebrows rose, urging her to go on.

"Detailed and all-encompassing information on the entire Detroit ring and how they're stealing money from your pocket. Especially how they recently stole your missing three shipments, blamed it on the FBI and have been inflating their numbers."

She saw it. The twitch where he'd chewed on the inside of his lip for a brief second. The narrowing of his lips and the muscles that tightened in his jaw.

Gianna opened her water bottle taking a brief sip and pinning him with her eyes. She watched the information swirl around in his mind.

D'Angelo leaned forward and motioned for her to do the same. Gianna leaned toward the table. His slight grin didn't touch his eyes.

"What would stop me from just taking the information, killing you, the man you sent, *the woman who is on her way there now*, and keeping the girl?"

Gianna cleared her throat.

If he knew about Kirin, then the contact was a double cross. How would she get the info to her? *God.* She'd sent her into the belly of the beast with someone she couldn't trust. D'Angelo's gaze bore into her. He waited patiently for an answer. What truly was her bargaining chip?

In the end, it was a stroke of dumb luck or genius that she'd given the crown royal bag to Kirin.

"Of course I was smart enough to have gained access to *both sides* of the information."

D'Angelo looked stunned. He sat back in his chair and stared at her for a beat.

"That's a bluff."

Gianna shrugged, "Maybe. But do you want to take that chance? How would Leo, your frenemy, act if he had all *your* information? From stats and numbers and cash, to pick up locations, hand signals and names, pictures, and fingerprints of everyone on the inside. Think about that for a minute. If I don't return home with my girl and the man I hired and anyone else involved, in twenty-four hours, both packages are sent. If I arrive safely, only one is mailed. To you."

Without missing a beat, he asked, "And how would someone like *you* have access to information like that?"

Never breaking eye contact, she thought about the proper way to say this without incriminating herself. This information she was offering him was intel that Steve would give his eyeteeth for, and she knew it. Here's where she waffled that precariously fragile line between doing what was right and doing what she needed to do to save a girl.

Her girl.

Finally, she answered as vaguely as possible. "Let's just say that a certain congressman had a smile on his face for days afterward."

Gianna watched him.

If he was a cartoon character, steam would be visibly rising from his ears and a train whistle would be going off. But then, he smiled. One of those grins that told her his plan went deeper than hers.

It told her Kirin was in more danger than she knew.

With her peripheral on high alert, she turned slightly to look down below at the clouds covering the earth. She'd just effectively painted a huge target on herself. One that both feuding sides of this trafficking ring would know about shortly. Sides that she alone knew had a long and sordid past of a love/hate relationship.

Sometimes, it's in the small details that you can really turn the heat up.

But now, her bargaining chip was out in the open and she'd hoped she'd moved her chess pieces in just the right order.

She hoped she hadn't doomed them all.

Chapter Twenty-Six

Knoxville, TN

"You're lying." RD whispered incredulously.

Her jaw had fallen open when he'd told her. Then her face began turning red. Damn if she wasn't cute when she was angry. She cut her gaze at him, trying to determine if he was serious. He didn't blame her. It sounded like a hoax.

Back in the day, he'd been a jokester. Nothing in his life was worth joking around anymore, but even he had to see the irony in this one. Dry humor used to be his specialty. His friends used to say he had the kind where you had no idea if he was just messing with you or if he was dead serious.

Right now, he was dead serious.

She stared at him a beat then without warning began pushing him off the bench.

"Move. I gotta go to the bathroom."

He just grinned and absolutely was not moving a muscle. Pushing him to do something was like trying to move a house. A house that had no intention of doing anything he didn't want to. And for all his trim and athletic build, he prided himself on being strong.

She paused momentarily, pinched the bridge of her nose and said, "So, you're telling me I have the letters D and A on my shoulder? Like the abbreviation for *Dumbass*? Are you serious or just yanking my chain?

Bo was caught between the sheer humor of it and the seriousness of what the letters meant.

When the waitress rounded the corner and set their food on the table, Bo immediately took a huge juicy bite of his burger. It took him a good ten seconds to realize RD sat completely still, glaring, and waiting for his answer.

He nodded. After chewing quickly and swallowing way too much at one time, he spoke, "The initials of the main runner. The one whom you now belong to. You're his. You've been branded with his initials in case another branch of this clan wants to claim you, they cannot."

When her eyes widened briefly, he continued. "Yes, it's archaic. But it's the way things are done. If your description is put into the underground system and he wants you for himself or one of his team, then he has you transported to him, tells you what to do and you're his."

RD turned, staring at her plate as she ingested the information. She took a few breaths, nodded, and tore into her burger as if nothing was the matter. Like they were two friends just having a meal at a restaurant. Like she wouldn't hate him when he handed her over.

Like he wouldn't hate himself.

His phone buzzed.

His meddling cousin checking once more to see if they were on the plane.

Bo looked at the time, stood, and began searching for the waitress. She scooted out of the booth and stood next to him.

When he announced, "We gotta go," she nodded dutifully.

God, this was gonna suck.

Chapter Twenty-Seven

Kirin and David had walked briskly, side by side, toward the bus stop of the busy street. He was an old-world gentleman and offered to pull her rolling bag for her, but she wouldn't have it.

Her purse was attached to the bag and although he was kind, she didn't fully trust anyone. And besides, she didn't want to lose the precious items inside her purse. She wasn't letting go, no matter what.

David was a small man. A few generations older than her with white cotton candy hair, who dressed very plainly in khaki pants, sensible brown shoes, and a modest white button down. The only thing that separated him from looking like the rest of mankind was the gold tooth.

David looked at his watch, instead of his phone, then pulled a pack of half crushed crackers out of his pocket, offering one to Kirin.

She politely declined even as her stomach growled on cue.

He shot her a kind look and devoured the crackers as if this was his only meal of the day. David stood and bent into the wired trash can, stashing the wrapper at the very bottom of the trash.

Either he didn't want his fingerprints right there at the top, or he was a conscientious citizen who didn't like it when light pieces of trash were windblown onto the street.

When the black bus, adorned with a bright picture of two smiling newscasters, made a high-pitched squeal and stopped, David motioned for Kirin to get on first.

She lifted her luggage and walked on the bus, only to be stopped by the driver who didn't look old enough to operate a go cart, let alone a bus.

"Card?"

Kirin stared from the young driver, back to David, who pulled a transit card out of his pocket and handed it to Kirin. When she'd swiped it for two, she handed it back and found a seat.

David passed her by, even though she'd scooted over enough for him to sit with her. She stared straight ahead for a beat thinking that maybe he didn't want to be seen with her.

When she cut her gaze back toward the back, David sat in the last row that covered the entire back of the bus. Shooting her a kind smile, he motioned for her to join him. The bus was already rocking side to side, moving to its next stop.

She stood, got dizzy and sat right back down. The second time, more determined, she stood, ignored the slight feeling of nausea—chalking it up to not eating, and forced herself to pull herself and her bag back toward him.

When she sat, his eyebrows furrowed.

"Are you feeling well? You should've taken the crackers."

"I'm alright. Where are we going?"

"Are you married?" he asked, not answering her question.

Kirin stared at him for a beat. "No, why?"

"So, out of wedlock then?"

"What?" Kirin's voice was high like a dog whistle, and she could feel the color drain from her face.

"Dear, I'm from an older generation. My wife and I had two sons. And I could always tell the small signs when she was in a delicate way. Usually before she knew."

David looked down at his hands and then out the window.

"She died…A year ago…dementia. Right after our youngest son was killed in a car crash.

She didn't recognize me or our eldest son toward the end. Terrible disease."

David ran a hand through his white hair, then continued, "I wasn't the best father. I was absent a lot and she had to do most of the raising. I'm trying to make up for that now. But I miss her…"

His voice trailed off.

Kirin's phone buzzed. She snagged the phone in her purse, but the message from Gianna was so vague, it made no sense.

They know.

She read it twice, then shoved the phone back into her purse. When David spoke again, his eyes were misty, and his voice held a gentleness she couldn't explain. She had to focus on the man next to her. She'd take apart the text later.

"How far along are you?"

~*~

Kirin's voice failed her.

Hell, her face did too.

Never send a rookie into a poker game with no poker face. She'd expected and planned for all kinds of different scenarios and questions.

Not this one.

And lying on the fly was not usually her best bet.

"I'm...I'm just *fat*."

David shot her a tight smile, then faced forward, still talking to her, but more distant. "You're nowhere near fat. The signs I see are different."

Call it hormones, or just a brief moment of insanity, but Kirin stared down at her hands, dropped her accent and whispered.

"Nobody knows. Not even my fiancé. And I'm still getting used to the idea."

David continued facing forward, but a tiny grin erupted on his face.

"Thank you for your honesty. I wish you and your family health and happiness."

Kirin grinned back.

After a beat of the two of them staring straight ahead, David glanced down at his phone, eyebrows furrowed, stuffed it back in his pocket, then answered her original question.

God knew she was glad to be off the other subject. But now, his speech was more formal somehow, as if whatever he'd read made him angry.

"Sophy, penthouse, top floor. But there's something you need to do before we arrive."

"What?"

"Open your rolling bag."

"Why?"

"Just trust me on this?"

Kirin hoisted the rolling bag on the seat closest to the corner of the bus so that other passengers couldn't see. She unzipped it and her jaw dropped open.

She hadn't packed this bag, Gianna had.

Which left her with the question, what in the hell was G thinking?

Chapter Twenty-Eight

Bo took charge. He looked more like the intimidating businessman she'd first laid eyes on downtown. He snapped his fingers and the bill appeared along with two to-go boxes. He quickly paid the bill as she tucked their food into the containers and shoved them into their packs. Within a minute they were walking briskly toward their gate.

When RD veered off toward the bathroom for a brief second, she watched him check his watch, eyebrows up telling her to hurry. She pushed down with both hands motioning for him to calm down. He narrowed his eyes playfully.

Trotting into the bathroom, around the labyrinth of short walls designed to give the women privacy, RD grabbed the first stall she came to on the left. The bathroom was divided into two large sections with stalls around the perimeter and a wall of mirrors in the middle. If she hadn't been in a hurry, she'd have probably gone to the other side of the rows of stalls and used the bathroom there.

She hooked her backpack on the back of the door and shimmied down her tight pants. Finishing, and as she pulled them up labored footsteps shuffled past her door pushing what she could only assume was a janitor's cart. A worker, she assumed, came into the empty bathroom right after she did. The lady stopped in front of her door and knocked. When RD answered it was occupied, the janitor shuffled to the next stall.

RD slung the backpack on and unlocked the door, pulling it to her.

That's when all hell broke loose.

Stars.

Literally she saw stars.

As she had slowly tugged open her stall door, the worker on the other side whacked the door with force as if they were trying to knock it off the hinges. The door ricocheted back and smacked RD straight in the forehead with a loud thud. Damn near knocked her out. She staggered back a step. Her training kicked in and her arms shot up to protect herself. She tried to force her eyes to focus, when two large hands shoved her body into the small corner at the back of the commode. She got one good look. An old woman with lots of wrinkles eclipsed the doorway and stood over her.

RD blinked once before the woman lunged toward her and shoved one of her cleaning rags into RD's face.

Her gut told her pepper spray, but it was something much worse.

~*~

Bo ran a hand through his hair, then glanced at his watch for the third time in a minute. He could see the gate where they'd need to board the plane. They'd already called for First Class, Priority Boarding and anyone with small children or wheelchairs. Now, they were starting with the back of the plane and people were lining up.

Where was she? *RD, hurry up.* Although, he had to admit. He himself wouldn't be upset if they missed their flight, but everyone else, including his idiot cousin would descend upon him like a kid with a stick hitting a wasp's nest.

He watched the door. Several planes had landed and the influx of women going in and out of the bathroom made him dizzy.

Would she have run? *No.*

She was more hell bent on getting on that plane than he'd ever be.

He stepped closer to the door as the traffic in and out of the bathroom slowed. He watched a young mom come out pushing a little girl in a stroller and he stepped forward.

"Sorry to bother you, but I'm worried about my girlfriend. She's been there a long time and our plane is boarding. Would you mind checking on her?"

The kind mom nodded, "Sure. What's her name?"

Bo thought for a second. He didn't want to use her real name. Then it hit him.

"She goes by RD. Would you mind calling that out and see if she's okay?"

The lady nodded then turned her and her daughter around. After a minute, she re-emerged and shrugged.

"Sorry. Bathroom's empty. Maybe she already boarded?"

Bo nodded and thanked the woman but stared helplessly as his brain stuttered.

He'd lost her.

But how?

He had to think fast. It was then the part of his burger that he inhaled, tried to make a reappearance.

~*~

Chapter Twenty-Nine

As the plane circled a tiny private airstrip, Gianna scanned the horizon. Her stomach turned. She had no idea where they were or even what state they were in.

Her gaze flitted from farmland to forest, searching for any landmarks she might know. Lush green rolling mountains stood at attention and right in the middle of a gaggle of them, stood a pristine wide lake that twisted and turned for miles and miles as if it'd been drawn by a small child. The sun glinted off the water, blinding her slightly as the plane banked right.

Even from their elevation, she could see boats like tiny specks, a marina filled with vessels and even a few large cruise liners enjoying their day without a care in the world.

She found it ironic that she was in a metal tube five feet away from one of the most dangerous men of her time.

She could feel him watching her. No matter what she saw out the window, she'd need to fight to keep her face even and passive. Keep up the ruse that she didn't know where she was even if she did.

And that's when she saw it.

The one landmark that told her she was in Tennessee. When she saw Norris Dam, she knew, but kept scanning the landscape as if she were trying to figure it out.

Norris, Tennessee was a small lake community attached to a massive TVA built lake. From her house, it was just over thirty minutes north of her. The Wall Street Journal had even run a piece recently on it, stating that for northerners especially, this was the holy grail of posh places to vacation or retire.

The lake was well known for its clear, clean water and over 800 miles of pristine shoreline, marinas, ATV trails, RV campgrounds as well as high end, gated estates.

In downtown Norris, the tiny town named after the lake, there sat a small private airport, and circled patterned streets with 1930's homes built when the dam was first put into place. Most of the homes had been refurbished and sold to young couples looking to live close to the lake.

The marinas were filled with cruise liners worth more than her house and expensive fishing and speed boats. And the shoreline in some areas held lush green landscaped mansion after mansion, indicating this place was full of money. It was the hottest place to vacation and retire.

Gianna shook her head, chin high as she tore her gaze from the window as if she didn't care where they were. She took a sip of her water and locked eyes with D'Angelo who sat low in his chair watching her curiously.

"Do enjoy the theatre?" he asked.

"Of course."

"And do you swim?" he asked.

Gianna prayed he didn't see her eye twitch. Seemed like an odd question, but she'd bite.

"Not from this elevation, but normally like a fish. You?" She lied.

A slight smile crept up his lips. "Every chance I get. We're going to my estate. A few brief hours of vacation if you will. Will you be my guest today?"

She tilted her head and shot him a look. "A guest you kidnapped?"

He had enough humility to look down and nod, "True. But today, I don't want to make this about business. I just want to enjoy a day on the lake. Life is short, would you agree?"

Gianna nodded.

She'd been taken to his lake home for a day of leisure. What? This had to be a trap. Gianna went over all possible strategies as any good chess player would.

What could he possibly gain from this? Drowning her in the lake? She'd already told him if she didn't come back, both packages would be delivered, and the man in charge of his downline, who made no qualms about spreading the word he wanted him dead, would get all his information.

Getting on her good side or forming an alliance so that she'd call off the delivery of the information? Maybe.

Did he want attention, affection? That'd be easy, but what could he possibly gain from it? Then her mind drifted to Steve.

Steve wouldn't understand the things she'd been through. The acts she'd had to perform to stay alive. The lengths she was willing to go to save her daughters. How could she ever have thought that the golden boy could stand next to her and not look down on her?

She sighed. She'd admit she enjoyed the power of it when she was younger. But now, she had other young girls looking up to her. Ones that had been on the line to be sold or even ones that they'd rescued who'd been made to do bad things, her perspective had changed.

The plane circled and finally landed roughly. She watched D'Angelo's brow crease as they taxied toward the small tower. Two blacked out SUVs stood at the ready, waiting.

If she worked her magic right, she could get both Sam and Kirin home for their stupid wedding in two weeks. Get her daughter back and put this all behind them.

If Kirin kept her wits about her.

Chapter Thirty

Chicago, IL

Leo slammed his laptop closed.

The skinny hacker who sat on the other side of his desk jumped, but then quickly went back to hacking into airport cameras to see what went wrong.

Two women had gotten off the plane in Chicago, but one— the one Leo had wanted to suffer most—somehow vanished into thin air.

He'd promised the little girl, if she'd help him trap the operative spy coming to kill him, he'd help her find her sister. But that paper trail had been covered up by someone in government. His best hackers couldn't break the whereabouts of that girl.

But he couldn't tell her that just yet, he'd just have to put her off.

But now, his intel indicated that the one person in the world who knew too much about him, had undercut him and grabbed the tall lawyer.

D'Angelo. Stupid fuck.

They'd been friends once.

Their parents had been the best of friends. Leo had grown up poor but proud and D had been on the nicer side of Detroit. They both went to decent schools, played ball, and went to upscale parties. But deep down, they were always competing. And Leo always seemed to be one step behind D'.

He gritted his teeth. This was too far. D' knew that Leo wanted Gianna. He'd have to make them both pay. And with the other woman heading his way, he had the perfect plan to fix them both.

~*~

Kirin stared into the opened black suitcase as the bus bounced toward its destination. David sat next to her, hands folded in his lap watching as if he already knew what she'd find. She expected a gun, pepper spray or hell, *something* to defend herself with.

But this had to be a joke.

Or Gianna's subtle way of offing Kirin.

The big rolling suitcase was filled with rolled up colorful thin towels. No clothes, no toothbrush or overnight bag. Nothing. Just towels. Ugly ones at that.

Kirin unzipped all the compartments inside the rolling bag. Nada. Not even a stick of gum.

She unrolled all the towels carefully, one by one until she came to the one at the very bottom.

This one was different.

The towel itself was bright purple. As she unrolled it, first, one furry brown leg appeared, then a second one. Then a brown wooly belly, and one arm—the other one was missing. Right where the arm should've been, white fuzz spilled out. A smiling head peered up at her with one eyeball missing and two cute bear ears, one jagged as if it'd had a bite taken out.

The stuffed animal was matted in a few spots and when she pulled it out and put it on her lap, it was about the size of her hand. So much stuffing was missing, she could fold it over like a poster and make it even smaller.

Kirin glanced up at David, eyebrows furrowed.

He stared for a beat then shrugged, "I'd at least take the bear. But I cannot sneak you inside with a suitcase."

Kirin stared at it for a beat. Zipping it up, she untied the ribbon she'd placed on the handle and put it in her purse, then placed the bag on the bus floor next to the window. Then with care she tucked the bear inside a zipper compartment of the purse. It was a tight fit even for the small bear, but if this was some sort of bargaining chip that she didn't understand just yet, she didn't want to show her cards in case someone rummaged through her purse.

Kirin took a deep breath, then turned to David.

"What now?"

He scratched the stubble on his chin, "Now, we must get you inside the penthouse at the precise moment. But first, I have an awkward request."

Kirin's stomach fluttered, "What?" she asked cautiously.

"You need more makeup." He stated plainly.

Kirin stared at him like he'd lost his mind, pulled out a compact from G's purse, opened it and glanced at herself. "Are you kidding me?"

He shook his head no. "The women that will be paraded in today, will look way more like *professionals* than you do."

Kirin snorted. No way. Nobody could look worse than she did right now. She glanced over and saw the dead serious look on David's face. "And you need to beef up that accent."

Kirin dug inside the purse carefully. Her blue and yellow patterned makeup bag sat off to one side. Kirin's cell and new wallet with her new fake ID sat in the middle, and the purple crown royal bag was tucked under everything else.

She didn't dare pull anything out, for as nice as David seemed to be, she only trusted *most* of the people she was working with.

Gianna was now back on the *maybe* list.

Unzipping, she pulled out a small brush, eyeliner, mascara, 3 lipsticks, a tube of magnetic gunk that helped her fake eyelashes stay on, and several more tubes of face altering substances that Gianna had apparently stuck in there.

Holding the mirror in her lap, tilted toward her face, she tried to mimic the make-up that was already there, just making it darker.

It seemed hilarious to her that she'd completely forget how different she looked until catching a glimpse in a window or mirror. Finishing up by brushing out the dark extensions and curling them around her finger, she placed everything except the lipstick and the mirror back inside the bag.

Holding up the mirror, she outlined her lips, then filled them in, but something behind the bus caught her eye.

As if in slow motion, two cars jockeyed angrily for the space behind the bus. When Kirin closed the mirror and shoved it back into her purse, she noticed that David had scooted all the way over to the other side on the long bench seat and pulled his cap out of his jacket pocket, shoving it way down on his head, shielding most of his face.

He too watched the cars scrape sides and shove each other out of the way. Cars surrounding them were stopping and backing away.

Then, out of one of the car windows, she saw the tip of an AR.

Aimed at the back of the bus.

Chapter Thirty-One

Yellow.

Her mind registered only yellow.

And the biggest throbbing headache of her life.

RD had been knocked out. She remembered that much. She'd hit her head on the back wall of the toilet when a rag with cleaning solution—no…wait. A rag with *something* on it that caused her bones to go mush and her mind to flit in and out of consciousness.

But she'd come to several times. It was like watching a movie while falling asleep on the couch. She could remember parts of it, but then parts were completely blank.

In her dreams between consciousness, she was suffocating. Like a heavy object was on her chest and it'd been hard to breathe. But whenever she could get her mind to focus for a half a second before passing back out, all she could see was yellow.

Whatever had been in that rag was beginning to wear off and she was starting to make sense of things. Her hands and feet were bound…no nothing was wrapped around them. But she couldn't move.

Whatever material she was rolled up in like a burrito was stiff like a brand-new carpet but smelled like smoke.

RD lay on her back as panic rose in her throat. She was unable to move her arms as they were pinned at her side by the carpet. Claustrophobia was settling in.

Calm. She closed her eyes and breathed. *Remember your training.* Panic does nothing.

Cataloging always helped when her mind began its descent into terror. From the small amount of wall she could see and the rumbling of tires, RD had to be inside a van. It was dark outside, or the van was blacked out. Either way, she had to wait for her eyes to adjust.

Her feet and knees seemed to have more wiggle room than her arms and hips. The van hit a bump and the carpet threatened to roll. *No*. Not on her stomach. Then she'd really panic.

But then, an idea hit.

On the next bump if she used the muscles in her back, and pushed out with her arms, she might just be able to expand her space. She'd be risking a rollover on to her face though.

Plus, she couldn't see the rest of the van. What if someone was with her in the back, watching her.

Just then, two voices wafted toward her.

"...go and check." A woman's voice commanded.

"It's fine." A man with a thick accent said.

"Okay, but this is your deal if we show up and she's dead because she suffocated."

Through the road noise she heard stomping, coming toward her, and getting louder. The footsteps passed her head and headed for what she assumed was the back of the van. RD closed her eyes and waited.

The man picked up the carpet surrounding her feet and spun her toward the middle of the van on her stomach. She tried to breathe through the panic of her own weight and the carpet crushing down on her lungs with her legs up in the air.

She felt the carpet ease off around her feet and then he released her legs. They came down with a thud.

That'd be a bruise.

Next, he stomped toward the top of the carpet where her head was. Even though breathing was tough she tried to stay as still as possible.

With a grunt, he lifted the carpet and put her chest on his knee. This one movement knocked the wind out of her. There was no hiding her breathing. She gasped for air.

He seemed to panic a bit hearing this and worked quicker pulling hard at the end of the carpet to give her way more room. With her eyes closed, softly as she could, she continued to gasp for air, but kept her mouth open and slack as if she were still unconscious. Telling her mind over and over that she was getting oxygen. This would pass. Give it time.

136

Thank God, this time he laid the end where her head was down easily. Then he flipped her back over onto her back and stomped toward the front.

"Done," he said to the woman who obviously was driving.

As RD's breathing returned to normal, she wiggled her fingers. The space was still tight, but now she could pull a hand up and scratch her nose if she wanted.

She also had a better view of her surroundings.

She bounced around in the back of a white work van. The uneven cold floor was covered in dried paint splatters, dirt, and fishing gear.

When the man turned sideways she discovered he was a large Asian man who looked like the ninja who'd stood in the corner at Marble City Market. The more she stared and listened to his voice, the more she knew it was.

Was he related to Bo in some way? She'd bet he was. The woman driving was large and wore a sleeveless shirt. As she drove, one hand was peeling something off her face and throwing what looked like sheets of wrinkled dead skin into a small trash can between the two seats.

RD instantly gritted her teeth.

She'd know that bingo wing anywhere.

~*~

After checking the bathroom himself when no one was looking, checking the gate and the plane, Bo sprinted for the parking lot. God, he hoped she was okay.

When Bo called his cousin, there was no answer. Shocker. He couldn't report her missing, she didn't exist except on paper.

He did the only thing that he knew to do. As Bo jogged through the sliding glass doors and toward his car, he dialed his father.

"Ni hao," his father greeted him.

Bo revved his engine and continued to explain everything in fast Mandarin to his father as he backed out of his parking space. At one point, he hesitated, trying to decide how much to tell him. His father's health wasn't good, and he knew the man didn't need this type of stress. But his elder cut him off.

"And you knew this woman before this trade?" He asked in Mandarin. Yes, his father could always see through him. Knew him too well.

"Yes."

"And you're fond of her? Love her?"

Love was a strong word, but the thought of what she was about to go through or her being hurt during this mission absolutely gutted him.

His father didn't wait for an answer. "I put you in this mess. My brother's mess. I knew he was into something bad. Before he passed, your uncle told me of a buyer who has a house in Norris. I'll send you an address." His father said in English. "But Bo?"

"Yes, father?"

"These are dangerous people. Get her and get out. I'll deal with your cousin and fix this mess."

Bo drove as fast as his car would carry him. His father gave him two more bits of advice before hanging up.

God, he hoped he could arrive first.

Chapter Thirty-Two

It felt as if time had slowed.

The old man had yelled for her to duck, and Kirin had. The spray of bullets hit and lodged into the back of the bus, pinging loudly on the metal and the window, but it hadn't shattered.

The young bus driver hit the gas and radioed the police at the same time. He'd tried to swing the bus back and forth like a serpentine but was going too fast to do it effectively.

The bus groaned and screeched tilting over toward her side. They were only seconds from flipping.

David crouched down between two seats. Kirin glanced over, wide eyed. He motioned for her to follow him as he duck walked up the aisle. Kirin left the rolling bag, threw her purse across her body and followed.

The other passengers were screaming, arms and legs flailing around as the bus pitched and turned. Kirin's body had been flung, slammed against the seats, and even been hurled forward a time or two, landing on her knees. Poor David's thin frame had been flung around like a ragdoll too.

Kirin continued following him toward the front of the bus. It took all his might to haul his body up on a seat. He pointed for Kirin to take the one across from him.

The sounds of metal crunching at the back of the bus made her want to look up, but she knew better. She held on to the plastic seat as best she could. It felt as if the bus were running over curbs and scraping past telephone poles.

One loud crash made her entire body twitch, then a second one shortly after.

The bus driver looked in his massive rearview mirror, slowed the bus and told the passengers it was safe to sit up.

David sat up slow as if the ordeal had taken a toll on his body. The sirens were now super close, and the bus rolled to a stop on a busy street in downtown Chicago.

David glanced at his watch, shook his head, and motioned for Kirin to join him on his bench seat.

He leaned low and whispered to her, "Whatever happens, don't leave my side. We need to get off this bus and make it to the Sophy in under ten minutes or our cover is blown."

Kirin nodded.

Panic had set in, and people were screaming and shouting, pushing each other, needing desperately to get off the bus. David stood, grabbed Kirin's hand, and shoved his way through the people trying to convince the bus driver to let them off.

The young driver was standing, thin arms up and shouting, with the pull-arm which opened the door directly behind him.

"People! Listen. My protocol indicates that we stay on the bus until authorities arrive. I saw four cop cars in my mirror, and they stopped at the accident site. They'll send an ambulance and a few more cars our way shortly. Just have a seat and we will get everyone taken care of."

David pushed to the front and squeezed her hand as he spoke to the bus driver, "She's pregnant and about to vomit. We need to let her throw up in that trashcan by the curb."

The young man's face drew up in disgust as he looked from David to Kirin.

Split second acting, she captured some air in her cheeks, slapped her free hand over her lips and nodded rapidly.

The bus driver looked back at David, then at the crowd and raised his voice.

"Okay. They're getting off to vomit, but nobody else. We need to stay put. Let's not get me fired on my first day, people."

When the young man pulled the arm and opened the accordion door, David ran down the steps followed by Kirin. David smiled knowingly when he saw the rest of the crowd bum rush the driver and file out onto the curb, like a whole bag of m&m's spilled on the floor.

David and Kirin sprinted off to a side street as David pulled out his phone and dialed.

"Need a car. Now. On my location."

He hung up the phone and continued walking, holding Kirin's hand.

"You're bleeding. Your head." she pointed out.

He didn't respond, only kept walking. Limping slightly and holding one hand to the back of his head. Kirin looked around. If her calculations were right, he was herding them both in the wrong direction.

Something felt off.

They made four more turns away from the city. She'd dropped his hand several streets back and he'd looked at her questioningly.

When a car beside them screeched to a stop, Kirin had a choice to make. She could run for it and probably at least outrun the old man, getting herself to the Sophy to finish out her mission. Or she could trust that he was indeed taking her there.

She took three steps past the car as David stopped and opened the back door for her.

"Terhune?"

This made her stop. She stared at the ground for a beat, then turned. Their eyes locked. The kind old gentleman's gaze had returned.

"I'll get you there on time, I promise." he promised, genuinely.

Kirin hesitated, weighing her options. After a beat, she turned, walked toward him, and climbed into the backseat of the car.

She prayed it was the right thing to do.

Chapter Thirty-Three

D'Angelo halted her with a tight smile when Gianna reached for the door handle. He walked gracefully, yet powerfully, like a big cat around the front of his black Maserati. When he reached her side, he opened the door and held out his hand.

Something in the back of her mind told her this wasn't his norm. She'd heard the rumors. An unstable, volatile man with an explosive temper. A loaded pistol. He'd been known to come unhinged and end someone on sight if they looked at him the wrong way.

And the rumor was, even if he didn't kill right away, he'd have them murdered later.

Fully ingrained in the mafia, the drug distribution side, and the trafficking business, and yet, she'd never seen pictures or even rumors of this side of him. Human. Walking around in high society as if he was someone. As if somehow, he truly belonged.

She placed her fingertips into his outstretched hand and stood carefully guarded, keeping her mind sharp and her expression unaffected.

The estate that sprawled out before her was, even for her standards, jaw dropping. She'd play the part of unamused, just as she had when they'd driven through the gated entrance.

A tall stone wall was attached on each side of the gate, backed by towering pine trees meant to deter the view of anyone driving by so they couldn't see the long tree lined driveway or the majestic house from the road.

D'Angelo had glanced over at her then. She had noticed how he seemed more boyish here. Grinning at her to see if she was impressed.

She cut her gaze toward him now and nodded, thanking him for helping her out of the car. She could appreciate an elegant estate, even if she was being held against her will.

The driveway was thin, immaculate, and shaded as if in a movie. It widened closer to the house and became cobblestone instead of smooth concrete. A circle drive in front of the home made it seem more like pulling up to a country club than a home on the lake.

The two bodyguards had trailed behind them in a Crown Vic with the luggage. When they arrived, D'Angelo spoke to one of them, low so she couldn't hear, then pointed toward a window upstairs. She watched as the man hauled her suitcase up to the room. If he rummaged through it, he'd find her gun. If she were lucky, he'd place the bag inside her room and leave.

The estate was mostly white with two warm wooden doors that together made one large arch. It resembled a vast Charleston plantation with multiple levels and sleeping porches as long and wide as a trailways bus. The home loomed over them. The grounds were covered in petite, expertly manicured bushes, and flowers.

The only exception was a phenomenal looking blue tree anchoring on one side of the walkway. Gianna stopped to stare at it. She'd never seen anything so beautiful. It was delicate and yet strong looking and the prettiest shade of light blue. A gardener was trimming it and nodded briefly at the ground, backing away when he saw Gianna staring at it.

"It's a Blue Chinese Wisteria Tree," D'Angelo said.

"Beautiful," Gianna whispered to herself. "I think I'll buy one for my home."

D'Angelo smiled, "No need. I'll have one sent over. A present."

Something in the way he said it made her feel uneasy, but she couldn't quite explain why. The gardener, never looking either of them in the eye, continued trimming the tree.

D'Angelo made a motion for her to walk down the path toward the front door. As soon as they stepped onto the porch, the ten foot wooden door opened, and an attractive young woman dressed in an old world black and white maid's costume stepped out. She smiled at Gianna warmly then lowered her eyes to D'Angelo.

He walked past as if he hadn't noticed her, then passed Gianna and led her into a large formal dining room where a spread of food waited for them. A young butler, also dressed in black, nodded kindly at Gianna and held out a chair for her. He laid a napkin demurely across her lap. She couldn't help but notice that the young man lowered his eyes when D'Angelo walked past him to sit, just as the woman had.

Gianna waited as the butler held the chair across from her for D'Angelo, placed his napkin, then quickly took his place next to the sideboard where he stood at attention, staring blankly at the opposite wall.

D'Angelo pointed at her plate, smiled lightly, and began to eat. After a bite, he realized she wasn't eating and spoke without looking at her.

"I wouldn't bring you all the way here to poison you. Eat. We have much to do tonight as soon as our early meal is finished."

Gianna stared at it for a beat. He was right. It didn't do much for him to poison her and she was grateful for the food. Truth be told, she was starving. She couldn't remember a time when she was so hungry.

She dove into her food as properly as she could muster.

After they finished their meal and the servants left them, she straightened her backbone and asked the question that had been eating at her since they walked through the door.

"Do you train them that way?" She asked sipping her water.

He turned to face her, "To not look at me? Yes."

She stared for a beat, daring him to look away. Their eyes locked. "Why?"

D'Angelo took his espresso and leaned back in his chair, sizing her up.

"Truth?"

"Always," she answered, confidently.

"Dominance." He said the word, then took a sip of his drink, making her wonder if he planned to elaborate.

D'Angelo exhaled, then continued. "Humans are unpredictable creatures. If left undominated they begin to believe they can overthrow you. I'm always at risk of some attempt at my life, and I don't intend to have that threat here, in my safe space. Which is why, by the way, your luggage has been thoroughly checked."

He stared at her for a beat.

Well, that confirmed her gun was gone.

"Solely for protection," she said crossing her legs, "you never know if someone will be a *gentleman* the first time you meet."

She raised her water glass toward him, and he smiled.

"That's why you're here, instead of Chicago. Here, we're treated as we should be, like royalty. Here is our sanctuary. Nobody will bother us here. You'll learn the ways."

Just as warning bells poked at the back of her mind, the young butler walked out of the room and right back in carrying two tickets on a tray.

D'Angelo placed his drink back on the table and swiped up the tickets. When he nodded to the young man, he backed away without another word.

"Would you accompany me to opening night at the theatre?"

It took Gianna a full ten seconds to respond. *Seriously?* She sent a spy to steal a girl from his Chicago operation and he wants to take her out?

She swallowed, "I didn't bring anything worthy of wearing to an opening night."

D'Angelo licked his lips.

"We took the liberty. You'll find a wide array of gowns and everything you need in your suite. Your attendant will help you."

Gianna shook her head, "I won't need help dressing, but thank you."

D'Angelo froze. His eyes narrowed for a beat.

Then he shrugged slightly, stood, thanked her for the company and ducked out of a side entrance.

It took Gianna a full minute of pinging her chess pieces back and forth in her mind to come up with a plan.

When she turned, the woman who had let them inside the house, was waiting patiently to take her to her room.

Gianna stood and thanked the butler who gazed, wide eyed and side to side as if her speaking to him was not allowed. When the girl near the door stretched out an arm to direct Gianna upstairs, suddenly she felt like she was missing something that everyone else seemed to get.

As soon as she got upstairs to her room, everything began to click into place.

Chapter Thirty-Four

Chicago, IL

Sam had been "trained" three times.

Whatever they were putting into his veins made him feel stronger, yet muddy brained at the same time.

They'd started to trust him though. Not locking the door to his cell. Feeding him steak. They'd even showed him where the workout room was in the basement and allowed him to continue his pushups and weightlifting in there, supervised, of course.

He couldn't remember why he wanted to go home. Didn't care really. Couldn't remember a time without these people. Although something kept niggling at the back of his mind, when he'd try to think about it, he'd either get a headache or super tired.

His trainer had given him a shower bag with everything except a razor. He couldn't remember the last time he shaved, but after his shower, he wiped the steam off the mirror and stared at himself.

Stubble, brown with a touch of red lined his jaw. He wondered if he'd been injected with steroids as his chest felt bigger. Part of him kept wondering why they were training him, but when he'd tried to focus on this, frustration would set in.

Sam lifted a hand and started counting on his fingers. He knew his name. Knew that he was used as a kid to get things for "The Club," knew Sonny saved him, knew Gianna was crooked…or was she? He shook his head.

He remembered he was supposed to be protecting some woman, but damn if he could remember who.

He'd hoped the shower would help, but it didn't seem to.

A knock at the door. He wrapped a towel around his middle and opened the door.

His trainer stood like a house. The man never smiled. Never. In his baritone voice, he said, "Time. There're clothes in your cell. Put em on. Strap that unloaded gun on too. You don't rank a loaded one yet, but I want it to appear you're packing."

"Where are we going?"

"An upscale place. We're not finished training, but something has come up. They need us. Follow my lead."

"Got it." Sam turned out of the basement bathroom and into his cell. He did exactly as his trainer said and was ready in no time. Both men walked down the long dark corridor toward an open door.

His trainer gazed back, "You do exactly what I say, and maybe I can score you a girl tonight."

Sam smiled.

Then, when the trainer turned back around, Sam frowned. Something in his mind told him he already had one.

~*~

Norris, TN

RD knew she had to be dreaming.

She'd gone back in time. From being wrapped up in a nasty yellow carpet like a burrito, to having a maid's costume thrown at her and her own clothes taken away.

And it wasn't even a cute maid's costume.

It was long sleeved and a long skirt that looked and smelled like it was from a hundred years ago.

The angry woman, who appeared to be only a few short years older than her, yelled in her face in Spanish. God, she should've listened to her aunt Rosa more, because this woman spoke rapid-fire Spanish, and RD's brain translated slow.

She stepped into the skirt. It was rough like paper rubbing on her legs. When she pulled on the white collared top with a multitude of buttons, the young woman stopped her.

Coming around behind her, the woman gently pulled back the blouse and touched the bandage Bo had put on her. Idly, RD wondered where he was and how long it took him to realize that she'd been nabbed.

She hoped he hadn't gotten into trouble for not making sure the "product" had been delivered without harm. Just as she was thinking about Bo, the woman, without warning, ripped the bandage, tape and all off her shoulder.

RD balled up a fist on instinct and let out a yelp from the pain. She was immediately silenced by the woman spinning her around and shooting a stern gaze. The woman's unyielding grip on her upper arm, right by the seared skin was causing almost as much pain.

RD had already been warned that they were not allowed to make a sound and if she were to look the master in the eye, he would make an example out of her.

She was a last-minute replacement for the last maid who'd been warned and still thought it prudent to whisper to the butler in range of the master.

That woman was taken down to the boat dock and never seen again.

RD nodded.

The maid then told her that whenever the master was in need, it was their job to be at his beck and call. No matter what he asked for.

Which is why she was being dressed and pushed immediately into service. The master had two needs. One was his own and the other belonged to someone else. A woman.

RD was catching about every other sentence, even thought she'd asked the woman to slow down.

Her Spanish being so fuzzy, she wasn't sure which one she was supposed to be doing. After a few moments of listening, it was clear that RD or *Candy* as they kept calling her, was to tend to the other person. She couldn't yet be trusted not to screw up with the Master.

The woman, Felita, was assigned to take care of more of the master's *urges* than his needs.

After making sure RD looked the part and knew exactly where to go, she jogged into the bathroom, fixed her hair, spritzed something on her clothing, unbuttoned her top button and ran out of the room.

RD got a glimpse of herself in the mirror.

Oh.

Her hair and smudged makeup made her look like a hooker caught in the rain, whereas her attire made her look like she worked at Downton Abbey.

Quickly, she tied her hair up in a bun, wet her fingers and cleaned up under her eyes and sprayed some of the good smelling stuff in the air and walked through it.

Now. Now it was time to gather some intel.

She'd get to the haughty woman later.

~*~

Bo had followed his father's instructions to a T.

He'd dressed like a college student with his short shorts, t-shirt with the arm holes cut out down to his navel, Hey Dude's and a backwards hat. He'd rented a clunker of a boat. It'd taken him a few hours, but he'd floated right up to the biggest damn house on the entire lake.

Good thing he was into boats. Sabotaging the boat at the exact moment was no easy feat, but he'd managed it right before the boat had turned a corner into the cove and was visible by anyone on the side. He'd strategically placed three empty beer cans around the boat within sight.

He used the momentum to steer it directly toward the dock in front of the house.

Well. Could he even call it a dock?

It looked more like a small marina. Five boat bays, all filled with top-of-the-line crafts like a cherry red professional fishing boat that sparkled in the sun, a luxury white cruise liner that towered and stood five times the size of his apartment, a decked-out pontoon, and two more massive engine speedboats.

Past the boat bays was a long, professionally lit walkway leading up to an enormous two-story party dock. Up top was a sun deck complete with bar, strand lights and outdoor luxury furniture. Down below sat a large screened-in room with a full kitchen and beyond that, a large stone fireplace and an outdoor TV surrounded by couches.

A tall man in a grey suit stood guard, leaning against a pole, and smoking a cigarette on the elaborate two-tiered deck, watching as Bo approached.

Bo waved, "Hey, man."

The man's eyebrows furrowed. He didn't answer, but only stared, then tamped his cigarette out and walked slow toward the end of the dock where Bo's boat was rapidly approaching.

"Hey, dude, I need some help." Bo cupped his hands and yelled to the man.

"No." The man answered, turning so Bo could see his gun.

Bo played it off, innocently and yelled back, "No?"

"No." the man said louder.

"But I'm dead in the water. Know anything about boats?" Bo pointed toward the motor as the boat drifted fast toward the dock.

"No." the man repeated, then added, "Go somewhere else."

Bo lifted both arms and shrugged, "Wish I could man, but like I said, I'm dead in the water."

He'd judged the trajectory correctly. His boat was making a beeline for the dock, but maybe he hadn't taken into consideration the speed when he'd turned his engine off.

His goal was to at least make it to the dock and not be stuck out in the middle of the cove.

Unfortunately, it looked as if he'd judged the distance all wrong. His boat was going too fast. If it hit the dock at this speed, it might damage several boards or God forbid sink him.

Although now that he had thought about it, then they'd have to let him inside the house.

Twenty feet.

Bo ran toward the front and pulled up his lead rope, eyebrows up toward the man in the suit. He stood with one foot on the edge holding the rope out, ready to tie it off on the dock.

Not slowing, the boat sped closer.

Ten feet.

The suit man's pace quickened when he saw that Bo's clunker was going to hit.

At the end of the dock, he knelt and leaned over as if he was going to push the boat away before Bo had a chance to tie off.

Their eyes met. Bo had to take the chance.

Five feet.

Suit man gritted his teeth and held out both arms.

Two feet.

Without warning, Bo threw the wet, heavy rope too hard and hit Suit man directly in the side of the head. It knocked him out of balance and into the water. Bo jumped off his boat and onto the dock, bracing himself for impact. The full inertia of the boat hit Bo mid body, right in the ribcage. He struggled not to fall into the water. Planting his feet, he pushed with all he had and groaned. When it finally stopped, he tied it off and spun around.

That's when he was met by a very unpleasant man in a wet grey suit holding a gun to his head.

Hands up, Bo put on his acting chops.

He swayed a bit and slurred his words.

"S-s-o-orry about that." He laughed. "Didn't mess up your phone, did it? Mine's dead. I gotta call somebody to fix my boat." He smiled at the man as if it was everyday someone put a gun to his head, then turned and pointed to the boat.

The suit man's jaw tightened, "This is private property. You need to leave."

"Uh, okay." Bo said. "What's the address here?"

The man stared at him like he was a bug and didn't answer. He needed to change tactics.

"Dude, can you call me an Uber?"

The man shook his head.

"Can you tell me what road this is?"

The man bit his lip. "Kid, you got about ten seconds to get your shit and get off this property."

Hands still up, Bo's mind was clicking fast. He turned, jumped back on the boat, and grabbed a sling pack with a purposefully dead phone, three full beers he hadn't poured out, and his gun.

He mumbled something about the man being a prick as he walked past him and started walking up the manicured lawn.

The man whistled and Bo stopped and turned.

The man pointed his gun toward a small patch of trees. Bo followed his line of sight. Perfect.

He flipped the guy off, then ambled slowly through the yard and toward the trees.

If what Bo's father had said was true, he needed to get inside quick before RD bit off more than she could chew.

Chapter Thirty-Five

Chicago, IL

Kirin double-took the driver.

When one familiar eyepatch accompanied by one widened eye stared at her for a brief second in the rearview mirror before peeling away from the curb, she knew.

Joel wasn't the person who was supposed to pick them up.

He'd been following them; she was sure of it.

He didn't say a word.

David winced when he sat, then looked at Joel and asked, "Who are you, and where is Reginald?"

Without missing a beat, Joel answered, "He got caught up in the wreck. They sent me."

David stared at him angrily for a beat, then waved him off. "You know the drill. Sophy. We have four minutes."

Joel didn't stop for signs or people in crosswalks. He skidded around corners and pushed the pedal on all straightaways.

Kirin was grateful to see him but wondered how deep this ruse would go. Would he go up to the penthouse with them? She wasn't sure.

Out of habit, or to get into character, she wasn't sure which, Kirin took out the mirror and checked her hair and lips. She'd been tossed around inside the bus like an old sock and one glance in the mirror told her she needed a bit of help.

David stared out the window, with his handkerchief pressed against his head to stop the bleeding.

"Terhune," David whispered.

Kirin turned.

"When we get inside, you're on your own and so am I, understood?"

Kirin nodded. In the brief time they'd spent together, she'd found him to be kind, and honest with her, yet she could tell he was up to something, as if his agenda was different from the path she was on.

Either way, he'd shown her compassion when he didn't have to.

When Joel pulled the car to a screeching stop in front of the hotel, David opened the car door then quickly shut it. He stared at a tattooed man getting out of limo right in front of them.

David swore under his breath, then hunkered down a bit and turned to Kirin, quickly speaking, he pointed at them.

"See them?"

Kirin nodded. One short, skinny, thug with a beanie pulled low over his eyes and black sweats that hung low around his butt cheeks stood briefly then was flanked by two larger men whose gazes swept the area as if they were secret service. Their stern expressions said they meant business.

"Now, watch the women."

One by one, women younger than her but dressed like her piled out of the limousine. They seemed cautious at first, then, like a light switch, giddy. Not at all like they were about to be sold, but more like they were going to a party. But a forced party. Only a few spoke to each other. Most just plastered fake smiles and walked toward the building.

Kirin squinted.

All except the last one.

The last girl that got out was pretty, not trashy looking. Her clothes didn't resemble the ones in front of her. She wore a baggy black sweatshirt that said, "I'm only here for the food" with pink pajama bottoms with Anime characters all over. Her bored teenager expression was that of a girl being told she had to go babysit a brat instead of going with friends to the mall.

Dave snapped at Kirin, "Pay attention. We must get out quickly and mingle into that crowd to get inside. But the men at the front cannot see us. And, if you don't do it convincingly, the women will know."

Kirin gulped, then glanced at Joel one last time in the mirror. Counting to three, she and David both dove out on the passenger's side.

If they played their cards right, they might just be able to blend in.

~*~

Kirin stood. The night air had turned cool, and she shivered before quickly trotting toward the group of women with David holding her elbow. All at once, she lost sight of the group thanks to a gaggle of picture taking, guided tourists walking in front of her. They'd cut her off from the pack.

Panic rose in her throat. She pushed through the sightseers and caught a glimpse of the group of ladies. Sprinting, she was able to blend in just as the group came back together and the crowd of women hit the doors.

She walked in next to a young girl who had a plastered-on smile, but her eyes darted side to side in fear. The women who were more Kirin's age appeared more confident. She'd have to match their energy.

The only person who seemed to spot her sudden appearance was the girl not dressed like the rest. The younger one, who'd looked bored as she exited the limousine.

Kirin tried to ignore the girl's narrowed gaze. *Shit.* If she could keep that one's trap shut, she might just be able to filter in with the others. David stood toward the back and being small, nobody seemed to notice him.

The plush interior of the Sophy was all crisp linen and candles. The travertine floor with a beautiful vein of black ran out in lines as if it were hot black ink on a piece of ice.

Sparkling glass and warm wood surrounded the space. A glittering chandelier anchored the five-level high ceiling of the reception area.

Soft piano music played once you got past the noise of the doors.

They headed toward a bank of elevators. With so many women, they'd need to take two. The beanie-headed thug at the front and his two hitmen took the first open elevator.

The group of women nervously chit-chatted and split into two groups. Kirin made for the far group, noticing that the teen trailed her. David was in the opposite group.

Both doors slid open and the women all filed in. Once inside, Kirin slid toward the back of the elevator. Kirin glanced at the woman next to her. For some reason, the woman's purse caught Kirin's eye. It hung open and was completely empty. Quickly, she glanced at all the other women, who also had empty purses. Using the noise of all the high heels entering the elevator as camouflage, she fastened her purse together and squished it to her side to make it look as empty as the others. They'd probably been forced to empty theirs before getting into the limousine.

But she hadn't.

The teen stomped onto the elevator last and was the one to put in the code to get them to the penthouse floor.

Great.

She was part of them then. Maybe Leo's daughter?

Once she pushed the button, she shoved her way back to the back of the elevator, right next to Kirin. Kirin noticed that all the other women who were talking low to one another seemed to fear her, moving out of the way as she pushed by them.

Out of the corner of her eye, Kirin saw the young teen smirk. She couldn't help it, Kirin turned, and their eyes met.

That's when Kirin knew.

Same pretty dark skin and brilliant hazel eyes.

She looked down and saw the bandage she'd placed on the girl's arm that morning.

Had it not even been 24 hours?

In true teen fashion, the girl looked Kirin up and down with disgust, then rolled her eyes, whispering, "Your disguise is awful."

Kirin leaned down, and whispered back, "Sorry?"

"Whatever. You look stupid." The girl said quietly, turning her gaze back toward the front.

What the hell? She didn't look any different from the rest of the ladies there. Yeah, she felt a bit older, but two or three of the women were dressed almost identical to her.

Kirin lifted her chin and stared up at the numbers. She knew she should have let it die, but she just couldn't.

"Thanks. Nice bandage. And I didn't know pajamas in public were a thing." She whispered.

The girl's head cocked to the side as a small, slightly angry smile played on her lips.

"Okay. That's how you want to play it." She said, still staring straight ahead, but now with a death wish.

Kirin nodded without looking her way.

She very well might have just made this 100% harder on herself.

It didn't matter.

All that mattered was getting out the people she loved.

When the elevators opened, both groups stepped off and into a huge, marbled entryway. Dressed in an all-black too-tight hoodie, with an AR hooked around his shoulder and black sunglasses, stood a bodyguard Kirin recognized. He was one of the thugs with Leo they'd taken down inside the Eugenia Williams estate. She immediately looked down. The teen stared from him to her and back.

He stared over the crowd of women and spoke over the top of the noise.

"Single file. I said, get into single file! You're late. Customers are waiting. Leo is unhappy. Be warned."

Kirin gripped her purse and stood toward the back of the line.

The teen stood off to the side. It was as if she were a ghost. Nobody said a word to her. She pulled out her phone and began texting, ignoring everyone. Except Kirin. Every few seconds, she'd look over at her.

Kirin tried to shake the butterflies out of her stomach. She had to get out of this line and find Sam and the girl, but with little miss watchful eye over there, that wasn't going to be possible.

When the crowd settled down, a male voice from the other room yelled, "Arianna?"

Kirin's head snapped up, eyes wide.

The girl turned, glared at Kirin, and walked into the room behind the man who had called her name.

Oh, holy grail.

Well, she found one of them at least.

~*~

Laura had woken with a start.

She was finally home. Finally in her own bed after what seemed like a lifetime. The doctors had told her that people like her who'd been in a coma would sometimes feel as if they could go to sleep for days and never wake.

She'd felt that a lot lately.

Also, what felt like a house sat on her chest. It was guilt. Guilt for having a double life and not telling anyone. Not her husband, Adam and not her two best friends, Kirin, and Stacy. Nobody.

None of them held it against her. They knew she was only trying to do the one thing she could, to help these girls who'd been abducted. She knew they didn't judge her, but after finding out what they both went through, Laura couldn't help but feel responsible.

Someone had touched her hand. Was she dreaming? Or was this one of those things that weren't true, but her brain convinced her it was?

When her eyes fully focused, Steve stood at the side of her bed, with Adam.

She tried to sit up, but pain rocketed through her. Her muscle mass had atrophied and even with physical therapy, her bones felt like they were hanging on with rubber bands instead of muscle.

Steve motioned for her to stay, then held her eyes for a moment.

"What's happened?"

"Kirin made it to Chicago."

Laura held her breath, waiting for the bad news she knew was coming.

Steve pulled a chair up next to her bed and hung his head. "Gianna didn't."

Laura gasped. "What do you mean?"

"She was taken off the commercial plane in Chicago and put right back on a private jet."

"D'Angelo," Laura said more to herself than to anyone.

"Laura. Look at me."

Laura glanced up. For the first time since she'd known him, his poker face was gone.

"I need to know everything. Every tiny detail you heard about him while you were working underground. Even if it's small, and you think it doesn't matter. I need it."

Laura nodded, "Okay."

She stared down at her hands, thinking. Trying to make sense of all of it without her brain resetting. Remembering bits and pieces of conversations and wondering if they were right or just her brain making things up.

"So, a few months before the blast, there was this sixty year old woman who came into the underground clinic. She'd forced her way inside and she was adamant that we listen to her.

She wasn't there because she'd been trafficked, but because a young woman, who she feared had been trafficked, had gone missing. She shook the entire time she told us the story.

The two women had worked side by side for weeks as maids for some eccentric man in an estate on Norris Lake. The elder woman was just beginning to get the younger one to open and talk a little.

Then, like a flash, the girl disappeared."

Steve was scribbling down every word furiously as Laura yawned. She knew the drill. That meant her brain was about to shut down. She dug her nails into her thighs and continued, talking even faster.

"One evening right at twilight, the older woman was taking the garbage out and saw a black bag laying by the dock. She thought one of her trash bags had gotten loose and she went to retrieve it. She got halfway down the lawn toward the dock when she saw the master come out of one of the boats with a wetsuit on carrying a clump of blue flowers."

The older maid hid behind a tree and watched the master lay the flowers inside the bag, zip it, then pick it up and jump in the water."

That's when she knew. Knew that the bag had her young friend in it. He pulled chains off the end of the dock and disappeared under the water."

Laura closed her eyes.

"She said it was the biggest house on Norris Lake and that the front walk had a blue bush or tree or something."

Laura paused long enough that Steve probably thought she was asleep. But she was trying to categorize the items she knew. That's when it hit her.

Laura reached out and touched Steve's arm, making him stop writing. Wide eyed and in horror she whispered, "Steve?"

"Yeah?"

"I know what he wants. You have to get her out of there. Now."

~*~

Norris, TN

RD had been warned, albeit in rapid Spanish, which her brain decided to translate only a fraction of what the woman had said. But she couldn't deny, she'd been told the rules:

1. Don't look at the master under any circumstances unless *he* calls you by name.
2. Don't talk to the other servants in his presence, it makes him paranoid.
3. Don't go wandering into the West Wing. Nobody is allowed in there without his permission.

Well.

She guessed that the last rule would need to be broken, and quick.

Her intel indicated the man kept everything on a stealth, supercomputer. Locked and loaded. The information they'd intercepted told of corrupt dealings, transporting women, drug trafficking and bank rolls, but it wasn't enough to put a stop to the operation.

For that, she needed something stronger like an admission to murder, or a file or something, to indict him on manslaughter charges.

It was the only way to stop the ring.

And damn it if she'd come this far, not to stop it.

RD slid out of her room, careful not to make a sound. She needed to get her bearings. She'd been prepared for Leo. Prepared for Chicago, but here, she was flying blind.

First and foremost, she had zero idea where *here* was.

She walked down a long concrete hall with ten-foot white ceilings, dark grey walls, and matching doors. Lots of doors. But oddly enough, no windows. Classic servants' quarters in the basement. Small rooms, small beds, and plenty of them. How old was this house? The floors and walls seemed modern, but the finishes looked like an old world.

At the far end of the hallway, light poured in. She crept closer listening for any shred of sound. Nothing came.

RD took a deep breath and started up the stairs, which in the long skirt was more of a struggle than she thought possible.

The next level was brighter and noisier. She could hear a commercial dishwasher running and pots and pans clanking together as if she were in the back of a restaurant. She stopped briefly at this level. Most likely kitchen & laundry. Next to the opening of the stairs was a stack of white linens. Best to appear that she was doing something. RD grabbed the stack and began up the next flight.

When she arrived at the next level, cool air mixed with mint washed over her. Soft piano music wafted in from somewhere a few rooms away. White and airy was the huge room she stood in. She'd bet if she yelled out, it would echo at least three times. White marbled floors spread out like water, anchored by white couches, white flowy curtains, and the most beautiful view of an orange sunset glistening off a lake.

She stood for a brief second, absolutely entranced with the view.

Footsteps, hard and fast behind her made her swirl around. As soon as she saw the anger on the man's face, she knew she was in trouble.

"Where should you be?" The young man dressed all in black spat in hushed tones.

RD bowed her head and whispered back, "Not sure."

The man grabbed her by the shoulders and spun her around like a rag doll, facing back toward the stairs and shoving her up.

"Our new guest needs help dressing, and you should've been there ten minutes ago. Go now." He growled, then added, "Next floor up and third door on your right. Don't screw this up."

RD hurried up the stairs grinning to herself.

He'd told her to go to the exact floor she was trying to get to. When she started down the hall, the fourth door on the right opened quickly, then shut again. Slammed really. It stopped her in her tracks. RD looked around but nobody came out. Weird.

She arrived at the third door and gently knocked.

The door opened abruptly. Instinctively, RD gazed downward. That is until giant hands grabbed her and slung her like a ragdoll inside the dark room.

As her body fell to the floor, she heard the click of the lock.

Chapter Thirty-Six

Chicago, IL

Kirin watched the young girl walk into the main room of the penthouse. Both the entryway and the main room went dead silent. Slowly, the line began to move as one by one the women were being paraded in like cattle.

Kirin glanced around. Several doorways jetted out from the entryway, but all were closed, save one. It appeared to go into what she could only imagine was a formal dining room and adjacent to that, maybe a kitchen with a nightlight on inside. From where she stood, thanks to the small amount of light coming from the room next to it, she could see the outline of a table. As she stared into the darkness of that room, one tiny reddish-orange circle illuminated, then dimmed.

A cigarette. Crap. She was hopeful that room might be empty, and she could sneak out of line.

She was close to the end, but at the rate the women were walking inside the larger room, she only had a few minutes to execute a plan. Obviously, after all the women finished, they were led into another room to sit and wait. That would cut Kirin off from finding Sam and getting an audience with Arianna. She needed a plan.

Kirin pretended to adjust the strap on her purse and glanced over her shoulder. One of the larger men, with an AK strapped to him like a handbag, stared straight ahead as if he were made from stone.

A knock at the door, caused the large man to take his eyes off the ladies. This was her chance. As he turned, Kirin crept out of line and toward the dark room with the cigarette. She'd just have to take her chances with whomever was inside.

Four large steps and she was across the entryway and into the dining room. With her back against the wall, just inside the doorway, she allowed her eyes to adjust. The outline of a man, who didn't at all seem alarmed that a woman about to be sold just walked in, took a long drag of the cigarette. He didn't move a muscle. Kirin waited, but the man said nothing.

Finally, she spoke.

"I'm so sorry, but can you point me in the direction of the bathroom?"

"It won't help," the graveled, deep voice in the dark said.

"What won't?"

"You can't escape."

Kirin laughed nervously, "Oh, no. I just gotta pee." She'd said it in her best accent, and completely in character. Her eyes had adjusted well, and she could make out some of his features.

He regarded her for a moment, tamped out his cigarette slowly and stood. She watched as he methodically picked his gun from the table, shoved it down the back of his waistband. He moved systematically like a large cat as he came toward her. When he got close enough to her, quick as lightning he snatched up her arm, and held it tightly, leading her toward the kitchen.

It was right then, she knew.

He didn't smell the same. He stunk like a mixture of burnt hair and salty flesh. He walked with a bit of a limp and when they rounded the corner toward the kitchen, in the light of the small nightlight she saw his face. His eyes, normally beautiful and green, were sallow and sunken. His three-day stubble, that she loved, was thicker somehow and clung to his thinned cheeks. His hair was slicked back and not clean. And he wore a metal collar like a dog.

Kirin's throat burned. She dug her fingernails into her other arm to keep the tears from falling.

Holy mother of all things good. How could this man have changed so much in only a few days?

It wasn't as if Steve hadn't warned her.

He'd said, "Kirin, if they've tortured Sam, the part of his brain who could possibly recognize you, won't. You'll have to play the part until you can get him alone, or somehow force him to come with you, if he won't. He's strong, but our intel tells us, nobody comes out of there unscathed."

She knew what she had to do.

As Sam led her to the bathroom, he released her arm and opened the door. Kirin took a deep breath, plastered on her best smile and her fake accent, and turned toward him.

"Listen. There wouldn't be a way you'd want to slip in here with me, would you?"

Sam's eyes softened a little. His gaze grazed her up and down.

"Flattered. But you're not my type."

Kirin almost laughed.

"Oh, honey. I'm not talkin' about forever. Ten minutes. Give me ten minutes."

Sam watched her closely, then took a step into the bathroom. Kirin smiled. *Yes.* She'd get him inside and he'd have to listen to her. He locked eyes with her, and something seemed to click.

In a flash, his soft gaze changed from flattered to pissed. He grabbed onto the doorknob and said, "Just hurry up." And then slammed the door.

Well, that didn't work.

Conflicted wasn't even the right word. Boy, she was glad her fiancé didn't go into the bathroom with a woman that he obviously didn't recognize. But then again if he had maybe she could've broken them both free.

Quickly, Kirin flushed the toilet and ran the water, then opened the door.

Sam stood on the other side of the hallway, leaning against the wall looking casual and waiting.

When their eyes locked, a glimpse of recognition crossed his eyes for a second time and then disappeared. God, how she wanted to just hug him. She couldn't imagine the horror they'd put him through. But she knew she couldn't break cover. Not yet. But she'd need to move fast.

Kirin had to take a chance.

"What's your wife's name?"

Sam stared at her for a beat as if he might have had an answer, then shook his head and held up his left hand to show no ring, "No wife."

"Girlfriend?"

He shook his head.

That stung.

"What if I told you, I know what they did to you?"

Sam's eyes narrowed. "I'm not gonna fall for your tricks."

"No tricks," she said quickly, both hands in the air. "I know they tortured you. You have a life back home. One that's not in Chicago. A happy life."

Her voice sounded desperate even to her own ears. Fast and desperate. Anyone could walk down the hall at any second. She had to make him see. She knew she was unrecognizable to him. Hell, she'd be unrecognizable even if he was in his right mind. Which, he wasn't.

Narrowed green eyes surveyed her. He wasn't buying any of it. He shot her a look. She knew that look. When you're going to marry a man, you know when he thinks you're lying.

She had to act fast. And lay all her cards out.

"Look at me."

He obeyed and for a third time, she thought she saw a spark of recognition. But as quick as it flashed, it dimmed.

"It's me. It's Kirin. I know. I don't look like myself. It's a disguise.

Sam snatched up her arm and started back the way they'd come, through the kitchen. As soon as they entered the mouth of the kitchen, Kirin knew she had to do something.

Quick as she could, she yanked her arm free and grabbed him hard around the bicep. She completely broke character and whispered desperately, "Sam! Look at me! Really look at me. It's Kirin."

Sam spun his body around, breaking free and drew his weapon, pointing the gun directly between Kirin's eyes.

His hand was steady, but his eyes conflicted.

He stared at her for a beat.

"Look lady, I don't know who you—" It was then, his collar buzzed as if someone turned it up. She watched his lids slam shut as he winced in pain.

~*~

Just as RD's eyes adjusted in the dark, the angry click-clacks of heels across the wooden floor made her shield her face. When the lamp right above her head clicked on, she shielded her eyes. That is until a woman's whisper voice started berating her.

"What the hell are you doing here?"

RD gazed up and involuntarily smiled.

Gianna stood in a full-length cream-colored gown that looked like it was sewn to her exact dimensions. Her hair was twisted up and the matching heels made her look over six feet tall.

Gianna shook her head and extended a hand.

"Oh, you know. Just playing maid for a few hours."

Gianna bit her lip to keep from giggling as she spun RD around.

"You look...amazing." Gianna lied.

"Thanks. I don't look nearly as amazing as you do, *your highness.*"

Gianna rolled her eyes, as both women sat quickly on the side of the bed.

"First. Do you have a car?" Gianna asked.

RD shook her head.

"Shit. Tell me what you know." Gianna's demeanor had always been so cool and calm, but now, RD noticed, her hands shook, and her usual confident eyes were wide. She was out of her element here.

"The whispers I've heard indicated D'Angelo is looking for a wife. He wants a family. He's wicked crooked and I think you already know, a little off."

Gianna nodded.

"I need to access his computer. Do you have any idea where that would be?"

Gianna shook her head, "What are you looking for?" Gianna asked.

"Intel. I need something that will shut him down."

Gianna stared from RD to the window and back, then finally spoke.

"I already have the intel. I've had it since I left home."

"What?" RD almost yelled.

"Shhh!"

Lowering her voice, RD narrowed her eyes at Gianna and continued, "You mean to tell me that I infiltrated the damn organization, dressed up in this stupid outfit, got *branded* and you had the intel the entire time? Did Steve know this?"

Gianna stared at her hands. "No. I didn't tell him."

RD glared at her. She'd been through too much crap to not know the entire truth. She crossed her arms, expectantly.

Gianna turned toward her, "My intel came to me in an *odd* and dishonest way. I couldn't compromise his career and do that to him. And besides that, I couldn't tell Steve because he'd want me to stay away and go by the law and botch this all up. I couldn't…can't lose her." Gianna's normally strong voice and attitude faltered as she said it.

Normally, RD didn't feel sorry for the uber beautiful and rich, but she also had never had a loved one go missing.

"Who?"

"My daughter's older sister. Been looking for her for months. You remember that op a few months back where Steve's people pulled out the second in command of Leo's gang?"

RD nodded.

"She was there. She was there and she slipped through their hands. I knew I needed to go myself. But then, I hired an old friend to do it." Gianna's voice went soft. "And now, he's missing."

RD watched her for a beat. "Where is Sam now? And the girl?"

Sounding defeated, Gianna answered, "Chicago. Kirin's there too."

RD rubbed her hands through her hair as she shook her head.

Gianna touched her on the arm.

"I'm sorry you got all dressed up for nothing."

"You owe me a tattoo removal."

Gianna cocked her head to the side.

"Never mind, where is the intel now and does it only shut down D'Angelo's side of operations? Tell me you have copies of this intel."

Gianna winced, then whispered back. "I told D'Angelo that I do, but in truth, I only have one copy of each." Gianna wrung her hands, then continued, "Listen. I've got all of his financials on a thumb drive on the dresser, take that and whatever you find on that supercomputer and leave. Take it all straight back to Steve."

RD looked at her like she was stupid, then shook her head. "No, I won't leave without you."

Gianna grabbed both of RD's hands and held them, lowering her face to stare into her soul. "Your mission was to shut this ring down. Mine was to save Sam and Arianna and if all goes well, I'll have to grovel and thank Kirin for that." Gianna shot RD a tight smile and scoffed playfully. RD smiled back.

"So, the faster you get your ass up to his room and get whatever you can off that computer, the faster I can get out of this freak show and go home. But you gotta promise to get it and take it to Steve…"

Gianna's voice trailed off and her eyes misted over, "and tell him…tell him that I…" Gianna swallowed hard.

"I'll tell him," RD said softly.

A warning knock at the door startled them both.

Quick as she could, RD stood and pulled Gianna to her feet almost toppling the tall woman on top of her. She spun her around and unzipped her dress halfway.

Gianna's expression went from a 'what the hell are you doing?' look, to 'confident elegance' in less than a second.

If anyone doubted Gianna's acting skills, they were idiots.

When the door opened, RD stole a quick glance before slowly zipping G's dress while staring at the ground. D'Angelo strode through the doorway in a casual grey suit, smelling freshly shaved and smiling, contently.

RD knew exactly why he had that look of satisfaction on his face.

"Ready?" he cooed, speaking to Gianna.

"Yes. Just need to grab my bag."

RD snapped to attention and dove for the bag on the bed, holding it out and staring at the ground.

"Glad to see you've warmed to our ways." D'Angelo said, extending an arm to Gianna.

"I find it refreshing," she lied.

As they strode out of the room, Gianna stared back at RD. Her gaze darted from RD to the dresser and back twice.

RD knew what she had to do.

~*~

Sam crumpled to the floor. Kirin tried to help him, but he pushed her away. She knelt next to him. His eyes were clamped shut and he was holding the back of his head with one hand as if it were about to fall off.

"Sam," she whispered, "Come back to me. *I love you more.*" Kirin grabbed Sam's free hand and shoved a note inside his clenched fist.

"He can't hear you," A young woman's voice interrupted.

Kirin looked up to find Arianna standing over the two of them, smirking. She glared at the girl.

Kirin had helped this little twit.

And hell, flying all the way here to try and reunite her with her sister and here she stood holding the button down on a remote that was obviously causing Sam pain.

Without a thought, Kirin tried to quickly snatch the device out of Arianna's hand, but the teen was too quick.

"Ah, Ah, Ah," she said, pulling the small box higher and waggling a finger down at Kirin. "Not quick enough, lady."

Not taking her eyes off the wretched teen, Kirin swung her legs around and kicked Arianna's feet out from under her. The teen landed in the hallway with a thud.

Kirin dove on top of the girl and squeezed the hand that held the device, pushing her fingernails into the teen's hand.

"Get off me! Ow! Help!" Arianna screamed while trying to push Kirin off her.

Kirin could hear the footsteps running down the hall. Pinning the girl with her body, Kirin was nose to nose with Arianna. As Arianna's angry eyes locked on to Kirin's, she said the one thing that would stop the young girl in her tracks.

~*~

As two of Leo's bodyguards picked up Kirin, Sam and Arianna as if they were three ragdolls interrupting a party, Leo stood, arms folded and grinning like he won the lottery.

After all three were dragged back into the main room of the penthouse, Kirin watched Sam closely. One of Leo's bodyguards held Sam up as if they were friends. Kirin was glad to see that, but Sam's eyes were wide and staring around the room as if he didn't know where he was or why.

Arianna and Kirin had been dragged with high elbows and shoved in front of Leo by the bodyguard dressed in black who was not about to let go of them.

Kirin watched Arianna out of the corner of her eye. She prayed the teen had really heard her. Leo stepped close to the girl, smiled at her and relieved her of the device she was clutching.

"Great work, little one. You did exactly as I wanted and found the woman."

Leo looked older somehow from the last time she saw him. Pronounced bags sat under his eyes and his signature white fur coat looked a little worn. He still wore a good amount of lip gloss, but Kirin noticed his nails were no longer painted.

Smiling a tired grin, Leo spun toward the group. "This little powerhouse turned over the spy and found the bitch I put a hit out on."

He shook the device in his hands, "But watch out, she's got sticky fingers." He leveled a look at her before continuing. She returned it with a glare. "Men, she's going to be a force to reckon with when she runs this outfit."

Leo shoved the device into his fur pocket.

Arianna flinched. Maybe nobody else did, but Kirin caught it. Reminded her of Gianna adamantly turning her father down when he wanted her to run his company.

Leo's demeanor changed like the wind. He glared at Kirin. "Where is she?" he growled.

"Who?" Kirin asked in her most innocent and best Jersey voice.

"You know exactly who. Where is Gianna?"

Without breaking character, Kirin answered as honestly as she could.

"When we got off the plane in Chicago, there was a man with a neck tattoo holding a sign with her name on it. He already had her luggage, too."

Leo's face turned purple.

He stood and paced a few steps as the room went dead silent. Kirin glanced over at Sam, who was staring at her like he was trying to work out a mental puzzle. She shot him a tight smile then looked back over at Leo, who stood running his hands through what little hair he had.

Just then, the girl wriggled away from the bouncer and took a step toward Leo. Leo held up one hand and nodded to the question in the bouncer's eyes.

Arianna's fists balled as she spoke, "Your turn. I delivered the man to you and now this lady." She turned and pointed toward Kirin but hesitated for a beat as if she was trying to gauge Kirin's character. Arianna turned back to Leo and spat through gritted teeth, "I don't give a shit about the other woman you wanted. She's gone. D'Angelo won, *again.* I overheard you wanted her to be my mother. I don't need a mother. I delivered my end of the bargain. Now, where's my sister?"

Leo smiled his toothy white bullshitting grin. "Almost here. She'll be here tomorrow morning. It's already set. You two will reunited and if she's half the negotiator you are, she will rule this business right next to you when I'm gone, *daughter.*"

Suddenly, a loud shot was fired, just barely over the top of Leo's head. It lodged into the wall behind him.

Everyone ducked and some people let out an involuntary scream. When Kirin opened her eyes, the bouncer had released her, drawn his gun and aimed it along with the rest of the hired guns in the room, at one person. Even Sam pointed his gun.

The dark skinned, white cotton candy-haired elderly man stood in the middle of the room and held a twitchy gun-pointed at Leo's head.

When Leo raised back up, he began yelling, "Who in the hell do you think you are?" It was Leo's normally too-calm voice.

Several of the women who had just been paraded in, huddled together in one corner. Three buyers sat on the couch, frozen and looking horrified. The young thug began yelling at the old man.

David's gaze darted rapidly from Leo to the loud thug, to the four men who aimed guns at him and back.

Leo held up one hand and shushed the room. He took a quick step toward David, close enough that his gun almost touched Leo's forehead and whispered menacingly.

"You've just stumbled into a hornet's nest, old man. Who sent you? D'Angelo? That skinny mama's boy who couldn't get a woman without tricking her. Living down south with his crazy ass. Does he still think he's living in the 1940's with servants and shit?"

David's eyes flashed in anger. His white cotton candy hair had been stuffed under a hat and his hands visibly shook. Then suddenly, he was completely calm. As if some invisible force had washed over him. His gold tooth gleamed as he smiled at Leo.

"*My son* has deemed your operation to be corrupt and *inefficient*. We've decided to let you go."

Leo took a step back and cocked his head to the side.

"Old man, what? Get this piece of shit out of my sight."

One of the four men, the one who'd been guarding Sam, walked evenly toward David, gun trained straight at his head.

David didn't lower his gun. He glanced over his shoulder, smiled apologetically at Kirin then pulled the trigger.

The pop of the gun made everyone startle once more. The bouncer had seen the look in his eye and dove for the small man, knocking him down at the exact second the gun went off.

The bullet, initially aimed at Leo's head, hit Leo's right arm.

Kirin heard herself scream as the weight of the bouncer on the little old man's body seemed to break him. His head hit the tile with a thud. He lay motionless on the floor for a few beats until the bouncer picked up his arms and drug him into the foyer like a bag of chicken food.

Chaos ensued.

Buyers quickly exited, along with the thug and his bodyguards. All the older women except three, crept toward the opening of the large living room and peeked around the corner. Nobody noticed them. Slowly and carefully one by one they hugged the doorway and stepped toward the door. The three that stayed huddled together behind one of the chairs, spoke briefly then slowly spread out. Leo's people yelled to get him help. Leo whined as he bled profusely from his arm.

It was then Kirin realized David's gun had slid across the floor.

Kirin saw it.

Arianna saw it.

Both raced to grab it.

Youth and ingenuity are no match for experience and wit, with one exception—a foot race.

Arianna got there first and instinctively turned, aiming the gun at Kirin.

With both hands up, Kirin walked backwards slowly until she stood next to Sam. He turned and stared at Kirin for several seconds with absolutely no expression. She mouthed the words, *read it* to him and glanced down at his still clenched fist.

Arianna shoved the gun in the waist of her pajama bottoms and walked confidently over to where someone was bandaging up Leo. Without an ounce of fear, she looked him in the eye, reached into the pocket of his fur coat and drug out the device.

Fearing the girl would turn it up, Kirin spoke, "Arianna, no."

Arianna spun around and yelled, "I'm tired of this. Prove it. Prove what you said to me is the truth and I'll give you this."

Leo swatted his people away and stood, hands up to speak, "Hold on—" as if she'd been trained by the CIA, the young girl pulled the weapon out of her waistband and instantly aimed it at his head.

He immediately stopped talking, his face registering both anger and respect at the same time.

"You—shut up and sit back down."

He complied but looked as if he wanted to kill.

Arianna turned to Kirin, "show me. Now."

Kirin pulled her purse off her arm slowly and dug in the bottom. Her fingers danced around inside the velvety smooth Crown Royal bag until they touched a hard surface.

A drive. She knew it must be important, so she tucked it into the palm of her hand as she unzipped the side pocket.

The bear's soft fur tickled her fingers.

Kirin watched the girl as she pulled the bear out.

Arianna went from a tough as nails street kid holding a gun aimed at the head of the biggest trafficking organization that runs the Eastern seaboard, to a misty-eyed teenage girl in an instant.

"Unroll him," the tremble in her voice was unmistakable.

Kirin opened the folded bear revealing that he only had one arm.

Two tears ran down Arianna's cheeks and she let out a long breath, "Paloma?"

"Safe. At your new home. Waiting for *you*. Currently being protected by the FBI while we came to find you." Kirin motioned between herself and Sam. She could feel Sam's stare boring into her.

Arianna looked from Kirin to Sam and back. She shook her head and mouthed, *I'm sorry.*

Kirin teared up too. She nodded, then took two cautious steps toward Arianna and handed her the bear and behind it, the flash drive. Arianna instinctively handed over the box to Kirin, then folded the bear carefully and tucked him in the pocket of her pj's.

She glanced down at the thumb drive, then stared at Kirin with questioning eyes. Kirin nodded. As Arianna looked closer at the device, her eyes lit up.

It was then that Leo lunged for her.

~*~

Sam squeezed his eyes shut for a brief second, then reopened them, staring at the dark headed woman next to him.

The girl must've turned the electromagnetic thing off when she handed it to Leo. Sam's mind was clearing and the pain in his brain had subsided. It'd been several hours since they'd injected him and thanks to the drama unfolding before him, his fogginess had cleared up.

But what really kicked him into high gear was the note the dark headed woman slipped him.

It was in his handwriting.

He'd given that note to Kirin before he left.

The woman that stood protectively next to him, didn't look a thing like his fiancé, but he knew in his heart it was her.

Leo knocked Arianna to the ground and Sam instinctively ran to pull him off of her. It was meant to look as if he was helping, but make no mistake, his mind was clear.

~*~

Fat lying Leo had knocked the wind out of her.

Arianna gasped for air. His overwhelming weight in his ridiculously furry jacket was crushing her, and her damn lungs had picked that inopportune moment to quit.

Pulling and twisting the hand that was wrapped around the gun wasn't working either. She couldn't turn it, nor could she fire it. Both hands were pinned under him, one holding the gun and the other holding the stupid computer thing.

She'd gotten a glimpse of pretty handwriting with a fine point sharpie on the outside of the drive.

It read, "Files, D'Angelo Ardo."

She'd heard that name enough to know he was Leo's arch enemy, and she assumed this drive had things on it Leo would love to see, but without air, she couldn't even tell him.

His eyes were trained on hers and murderous. He grabbed hold of both her forearms and pushed himself up to sit on her stomach.

At least now she could breathe.

"Wait," she squeaked out, but he wasn't listening.

"You little double-crossing bitch, Ima end you right now." Leo said through gritted teeth.

It was no use. She was gonna die in this stupid hotel room and never see her sister again. Tears pooled in the corners of her eyes and a cry escaped her lips. Then, determination filled her soul. She *would* see her sister again. No matter what she had to do to make that happen.

~*~

Sam grabbed Leo around the neck with his forearm and squeezed. All the anger bottled inside was funneling to his grip on this man's throat.

He'd never killed. With all the chemicals they'd fed him that bogged down his brain, he knew that was true. Leo had wanted Kirin, the love of his life, dead. The woman who completed him.

He glanced back at her. Her hands covered her mouth and tears had made black lines of makeup run down her cheek. She shook her head.

The other bodyguards lifted guns at him, including the one who'd trained him. That big tough man's face looked like someone had killed his dog.

Leo dropped the hold he had on Arianna's forearms and gasping for air pulled at Sam's tight grip, but it was no use. The pushups mixed with whatever crap they gave him had bulked him up and he was damn sure not letting go.

This needed to end.

Now.

Sam slammed his eyes shut, gritted his teeth, and squeezed harder. He was tired of running. Tired of allowing organized crime to rule his life. He squeezed and waited for his innocence to end.

A pop pierced the silence. Sam froze. Even more shocking than the noise was the shock of the young girl's aim.

Only a few inches to the right, and he'd be the one crumpling to the floor instead of Leo.

The room fell silent, but only for a second. The three women had crept and spanned out across the room, standing behind each of the bodyguards while everyone else was focused on the drama in the middle of the room.

All at once, they began yelling, "Drop your weapons! FBI! Drop 'em. Get down on the ground! Now!"

The bodyguards tossed their weapons to the floor. Sam leaned down and relieved the gun from the girl. Her body was like a statue, frozen in the position of shooting Leo. He shoved the gun in his waistband and offered a hand to Arianna. Without hesitation, she stood, and he pulled her to him. Her young face was worn and weary and she shook like an earthquake had a hold on her legs.

Just like Kirin had when he'd saved her in the parking lot from the robber.

Sam held her as she began to cry.

The room looked like someone had bombed it. Sirens rang out on the streets below.

Kirin took two healthy steps toward one of the women holding a gun to a bodyguard's head, and when the woman's gaze snapped up angrily to meet hers, Kirin halted and her hands rose in surrender.

"Terhune?" the woman asked.

"Yes," Kirin answered, hands still up.

"You're free to go but exit quickly. You never saw us. This was unsanctioned." And then to her team, she yelled, "Operation Redeeming, move out."

Kirin nodded in appreciation, then ran to Sam and Arianna.

"Follow me, now."

Sam guided Arianna as they followed Kirin through the foyer. When she passed the little old man's body Kirin stopped, stooped, and touched him on the shoulder. After a beat she wiped her eyes and ran through the door that was already swung open.

Sam yelled for Kirin to stop. She turned and stared at him like he was crazy.

But Arianna had wriggled away. She ran back into the living room where Leo's dead body lay. Sam sprinted behind her.

The young girl bent over, picked up the little brown bear that had fallen out of her pocket, when she'd been tackled, then turned and ran right back to Sam, grabbing his hand.

Kirin nodded then, when they'd caught back up to her, she turned and ran for a sign that read, STAIRS. She'd found a set of cold, concrete stairs and he prayed they led outside. He was sure the penthouse and half the Sophy was already crawling with police.

Kirin yelled like a drill sergeant for all to run to the bottom. He'd never seen her move so quickly. Sam and Arianna trailed behind her a few steps.

When they got to the bottom floor, they found two exit doors; the first said, LOBBY while the other indicated that an alarm would sound if pushed, which meant it led outside.

Sam looked around. How in the hell was he going to get the three of them through downtown Chicago to safety.

~*~

Kirin didn't think. She just pushed open the door with the alarm. The shrill sound made Arianna grab her ears. She searched around as she shoved open the door, then ran. Sam and Arianna, for their part, followed her blindly. Kirin pushed the door open and ran.

The door led out to a back alley lined with dumpsters. Kirin quickly decided for whatever reason, to head to the right. She sprinted, feeling older than her age, in high heels.

When they came to an end, the alley opened up to a very busy street. She told Sam and Arianna to wait in the shadows as she walked to the corner, hailing a cab.

Except what pulled up wasn't a cab.

~*~

Kirin had a knack at falling into trouble backwards, of that, he was sure. If Sam hadn't been so happy to finally realize the dark headed woman was her, he'd have been pissed. She clearly had zero regard for her own safety. Hell, she came to Chicago *alone* to take on the establishment and save him.

Then again, he'd done the same thing to save the girl.

As Kirin stood on the street corner, one arm raised to hail a cab, amid whistles and a few men walking by who looked her up and down, Sam smiled.

His woman was badass.

But then, Kirin flagged down the sketchiest looking cab driver, driving the biggest hunk-of-junk, spray-painted minivan he'd ever seen.

When the sliding door flung open, Kirin jumped into the middle seat as Sam handed Arianna to her and she buckled them both in. Sam slammed the sliding door and dove into the front seat.

The weirdo cab driver, with an eyepatch, pulled away from the curb and sped away like they'd just robbed a bank.

When he did, he smiled at Sam like he wasn't wearing pants.

It took Sam's mind about three seconds to realize it was his brother. He patted Seth's arm and exhaled for the first time in what felt like a week.

On Arianna's request, Kirin dug the box out of her purse. Arianna's small cold fingers, using the key that was hidden inside the device, unhooked the metal collar around Sam's neck. He turned to see her pitch the collar to the floor, then she laid her head down on Kirin's lap and closed her eyes.

Undeniable relief and emotion hit Sam all at once.

Sam put his face in his hands. All that he'd been through, just to have a normal life, ran through his mind. Most men took for granted their normal day to day lives. He vowed right then and there not to waste one moment. Promised himself they'd live out the rest of their days just holding on to one another.

Sam wiped his face, then looked back at Kirin. She stroked Arianna's hair. As their eyes met, a tear slid down Kirin's cheek.

~*~

Gently, so as not to disturb Arianna, Kirin slowly pulled her purse off her shoulder and wedged it open between her seat and the door. She pulled her phone out and typed three words:

All are safe.

After placing her cell back inside her purse, she dug around in the bottom to find the item she'd hidden.

Sam glanced over his shoulder. He looked at Arianna, already asleep, then back up at Kirin.

Their eyes locked and all the emotions of almost losing one another came to the surface. One tear escaped his eye as he reached a hand back toward her. Kirin took his hand, squeezed it, and nodded. A huge lump came up in her throat.

No words were needed. She was relieved to have him back and prayed that after everything they did to him, he'd be back to the same man she loved.

Sam nodded down toward the sleeping girl and whispered, "I hope someday we have a girl."

Kirin smiled.

Carefully, she unwrapped and placed the positive test into his hand.

Chapter Thirty-Seven

Norris, TN

RD rummaged around the top of Gianna's dresser until she found the small hard plastic thumb drive. Immediately, she stuck it in her bra.

Giving the happy couple a few minutes to get downstairs, RD tidied up the room. It was also a good guise in case that idiot supervisor showed his face again.

As she hung clothes on hangars, she idly wished she could've gotten her hands back on her gun. If she had her gun she could find the information on his computer, add it to whatever Gianna had acquired unlawfully, steal a car, get it to Steve and save Gianna. But she didn't have it, Bo did.

Her mind switched to his sexy grin and that strong jawline that flexed when he was contemplating. She wondered if he'd gone about his day after she disappeared or if he'd searched for her.

RD shook her head. It made no difference, really.

She'd probably never see him again and that was fine by her.

Except, it kind of wasn't.

The evil woman who'd attacked her in the bathroom and the man who'd stood in the corner at the Top Golf suite were apparently paid handsomely to bring her in. Just another slave in the world.

She'd been tossed inside the lion's den and told exactly what to do. RD took one last look around the room, clicked off the light and headed for the West Wing.

~*~

Thick red carpet lined gilded walls of shiny gold. Since moving from Chicago, Gianna had never stepped foot inside the historic Tennessee Theatre.

When their limo driver dropped D'Angelo, Gianna and two bodyguards off, she noticed the theatre had an old world, glassed-in ticket booth that stood guard, uninhabited toward the street. The only way of knowing she was in the twenty-first century was the ushers at the door with barcode scanners.

Most of the crowd were much older than she and D'Angelo, but by far, he was the best dressed in the place. Most of the opening night attendees' attire were made up of suits and nice church dresses.

D'Angelo was in tails and Gianna wore a floor length cream colored, sequined gown with matching heels.

It was a nice dress, but the only thing she was truly grateful for was at least it wasn't white.

A closet full of chosen dresses was what she discovered in her room. And almost all were long, white gowns. The cream colored one was the only one with any color.

She'd opened the closet door and stood with her mouth open. It looked like a bridal shop.

That should've been her clue.

Before ascending up the wide, carpeted stairs toward the premium box seats, D'Angelo stopped in front of a photographer set up with a piece of the stage prop for the play.

Gianna thought it odd, but when D'Angelo nodded toward it and smiled that male model grin, she automatically walked over for a picture with him.

He'd placed his hand on the small of her back to lead her there and she immediately thought of Steve. D'Angelo's hands felt very different from Steve's strong hands. Something in the pit of her stomach twisted. She'd much rather have been at the theatre with *him*.

After the photographer finished, D'Angelo insisted she have her photograph taken alone. It was an uncomfortable request, but she'd walked the red carpet a time or two. She knew how to get a good picture.

As she stood there reading his body language, and smiling for the camera, something clicked. He looked expectant. As if this picture meant more.

When they finished, D'Angelo grasped her hand and led her up the stairs toward their seats.

"Thank you for taking me to the theatre. I haven't been in years." Gianna crooned as if she hadn't been forced to go.

D'Angelo smiled, "I'm happy that you enjoy the finer things in life."

As they stepped behind the curtain into their box seats, an usher handed her a playbill.

"Taming of the Shrew?" Gianna turned, one hand automatically landing on her hip, and leveled a look at her captor.

He smiled, arms up and shrugged, "Not my idea. It just happened to be what was playing tonight."

Gianna shook her head and took her seat.

As the orchestra warmed up and people mingled below, an usher brought up a bottle of wine, uncorked it and poured a glass for D'Angelo. He swirled it and smelled it, nodding.

Another was poured and handed to Gianna. She held the glass for a long time without taking a sip. D'Angelo rolled his eyes and made a big show of drinking his so she would drink hers.

One of his knees bounced as if he were nervous or excited. Without thinking, she reached over and put a hand on his knee briefly to stop the bouncing.

When he turned and looked at her, he smiled. Probably the most genuine of grins since she climbed the stairs to his aircraft.

D'Angelo took a sip, never taking his eyes off her and asked, "We have a few minutes, mind if I ask you a question?"

"Sure," Gianna answered cautiously.

"How do you feel about children?"

"I love mine, if that's what you're asking." She stared right back at him. To his credit, he showed no emotion.

"And how many do you have?"

Gianna thought for a second, "One in hand, the other on the way."

He nodded. A twitch of his eyebrow told her he might know more than she did.

"What if I told you that I can get her to you?"

Gianna hesitated, then spoke, "I'd be interested in that."

One of his bodyguards tapped him on the shoulder and handed him a cell phone. D'Angelo excused himself and went out in the hallway to take the call.

This might be her chance. Gianna pulled her purse into her lap. The bodyguard who guarded the door behind her, stood feet wide and staring straight ahead like a statue. She pulled out her compact mirror and with one hand checked her reflection. Tilting the mirror up, she watched the guard. Closing the mirror, she scooted forward and gazed down at the orchestra with feigned interest.

If she only saw just one person she knew, she might not feel so alone.

This man was bipolar as they came with a layer of rage just under the surface. She could sometimes see it in his eyes. But for a man rumored to kill at a whim, he'd outwardly shown that he was the perfect, classy gentleman. When D'Angelo returned, however, she saw the anger. His face was flushed beet red and his jaw tight. Anger permeated off his body. He stared down at her for a beat as if he'd enjoy choking the life out of her, then seemed to remember himself. He stalked toward her, calmly and leaned down.

"Something has happened, and it appears we cannot stay. Please accept my apology."

Gianna nodded and stood.

Everything in her body didn't want to follow him.

Maybe Kirin had succeeded. Maybe Steve had found her and was in the audience. This caused her heart to beat faster. Until she realized that was just a fantasy.

With no gun and no cell phone and zero power, she was going to have to fight her own way out of this the old-fashioned way.

Gone were the hand holding and kind eyes. This man was enraged. He stomped down the red carpeted steps, with Gianna a few behind him and the guards right on her heels, pushing her to go faster.

When she reached outside, the cool air hit her. She stopped for a moment, breathing it in. Gianna refused to believe after all she'd been through that this might be her last glimpse of freedom.

In a perfect world, RD had found something, made it to Steve and he'd be waiting for them as soon as they arrived back at D'Angelo's estate.

That is if she survived the limo ride back.

~*~

RD crept down a long hall. At the end was a large, hand carved, wooden double door and next to it on the wall, a flaming sconce as if she were headed into a castle. It was the oddest-looking thing to find in a residential home.

Of course, the doors were locked tight. But RD had a trick up her sleeve or in her case, *in her shoe.*

The one thing nobody checked was her black sneakers. They were her favorite and they held secrets.

She prided herself on being able to crack any door lock, anywhere. It was her late father who'd suggested, when she'd told him of her desire to join the FBI, that she'd always have a plan B, C and D at the ready.

RD pushed a button on the inside sole of her shoe and when she did a compartment shot out on the other side with her set of tools: a small rake pick, fake credit card, bobby pin, and assortment of small eyeglass tools along with one long skinny rod, the depth of the shoe.

Immediately, she set to work, pulling, and pushing to see where the tumblers were. It wasn't the hardest lock she'd ever picked, but something seemed off about it. Cautiously, she checked the door frame for any signs of an alarm and found none.

She knew at some point the nosy supervisor would realize that D'Angelo and Gianna were gone, and she was nowhere to be found. He would come looking for her.

With quick, nimble fingers she got to work, but kept one ear trained on the long hallway behind her. Using two of the tools, she bent and quickly searched the inside of the lock for the mechanism.

The flame just above her head popped and hissed and several times she turned to make sure she was alone. Finding the flat part of the mechanism, she pushed but it wouldn't engage.

RD tried twisting the handle while engaging the plate, but it wouldn't budge. She knew it had to be something easy. She stood for a second to go at her problem differently. Then it hit her.

She lifted the door handle but was unable to keep it there and utilized both hands to push the tumbler and turn the knob counterclockwise. Crouching over and standing on one foot while lifting her knee to apply pressure from underneath, was the epitome of an uncomfortable circus trick. But this time she heard the click. The door, however, still wasn't unlocked.

Leaning against the door frame this time for balance, she took a breath and tried again. This time the door clicked and released.

She stood tall, lowering her knee, and smiled, proud of herself. Tucking the tools temporarily into her pocket she turned the handle slowly.

Without warning, strong hands from behind covered her mouth and shoved her body forward catapulting her into the room.

~*~

Bo narrowly avoided the right hook he knew would come. When the wild, beautiful eyes recognized him, he took a step back with both hands up.

The door had swung open and slammed shut loud enough to wake the dead.

RD whispered harshly, "What the hell are you doing here?"

He lowered his hands and took a step toward her, searching her eyes for a beat, "I missed you."

She stepped closer, invading his space and smiled as if he'd told her he loved her. Finally, she laughed, "You're an idiot."

Bo put his hands on her waist and nodded, "probably."

She stepped closer into his arms and reached up, grabbing his collar. "*What* are you wearing?"

Bo smiled, stepped back and then pretended to be hurt by her question, "It's my disguise. I'm a butler."

Three loud bangs caused them both to jump. Their reunion would have to wait.

When RD's gaze quickly swept the room, wide eyed, he knew she was looking for something specific. The only light in the room radiated from a computer screen.

"What do you need?" he whispered.

"Time," she answered, pushing past him when she spotted the alcove with a desk and computer.

Tenacious. The woman was tenacious.

Bo turned and silently placed his back against the door, surveying the room. An ugly ornate poster bed the size of his apartment anchored the middle of the suite. Thick purple covers were disturbed as if the occupant had just gotten out of bed. The suite itself was the size of two apartments. Three doors graced the walls; the one he had his back to, one that led to the bathroom and what was probably a dressing room or a closet as he could see the reflection of a mirror, and a third one that looked like a commercial outside door.

Keys rattled on the other side of the door he was protecting.

"Who is in there?" The butler on the other side yelled. Panic rang out in his voice.

Quickly, Bo scanned the room and found it. He jogged across the expanse, grabbed a hard back chair, and trotted back. When he reached the door, he shoved the chair back under the door handle and answered.

"Uh. It's me. I can't get out...is there some trick to this door?"

Bo could imagine the young butler's face turning purple. The man had already scolded him once for making too much noise when he'd first snuck inside and stolen the clothes.

"Oh my god, just open the door!" The butler yelled, shaking the door handle, then added, "If the Master comes home, you're a dead man. Nobody goes into his chamber. You need to get out, right now!"

At this point the man's voice was pitched too high and Bo heard his wad of keys drop to the floor. The man cursed, picked them up and shook them. Bo could tell he was fumbling to find the right key.

He glanced back over his shoulder at RD. The sun was setting on the lake outside and the room was dusky, but when the computer screen illuminated her face, he saw her grin triumphantly.

The door shook once again.

Bo checked the wedge of the chair. It was sturdy.

The butler shoved a key into the door lock. Bo watched in horror as the door handle slowly turned.

He pressed his body against the door for added measure.

When the butler unlocked it and pushed it, it moved less than a half inch.

"Do you have something blocking the door?" His voice was now low and menacing and not at all the hysterical high pitch it had been just a few seconds ago. It was low and angry.

"Not at all," Bo lied. "Is there something wrong with this door?"

Bo heard the cock of a gun.

~*~

RD used every hacker trick in her book. She'd cracked the code to get inside, but the files had to be so embedded it would take hours to extract them.

She glanced over at Bo, his back against the door, and using every trick he could to buy her time. But it wouldn't be enough.

Quickly, she made the decision to take the computer tower. It might not work and if the files were backed up in a cloud somewhere, they could easily be rerouted, but she had to try.

RD grunted as she quickly crawled under the desk and ripped out the wires from the back of the machine. Immediately the screen went dark.

When she pulled the last wire out, an alarm screamed out, loud and shrill, like a school fire alarm. She wanted to cover her ears, but she struggled to grab the tower and pull it out from under the desk.

Tucking the heavy tower under her arm, she ran toward where Bo stood, holding his ears. They had to find an exit point.

Bo yelled something at her as she ran toward him. She could see his mouth moving, but with the siren so loud, she couldn't hear. Three rounds fired outside the door were the only noises that pierced the siren.

She dropped the tower and it crashed to the floor, breaking part of the faceplate off it. Her arm wasn't responding as if someone had injected it with a numbing serum.

The force of the bullet knocked her back and she landed on her rear. Bo ran to her stripping off his outer jacket and shoving it against her shoulder. Pain ripped through her upper body. Dizziness blurred her vision. Shit. She knew she was losing blood fast. He pulled her body toward him, she thought out of kindness, but quickly realized he was looking for an exit wound.

The door rocked back and forth as if the man on the outside was attacking it with his body. Thank God Bo had thought to prop a chair against the door handle, but it didn't take a genius to know, it wouldn't hold for long.

"Take it," RD yelled to Bo, nodding toward the broken tower, "And get out. Go through a window if you have to. That information needs to get to someone who can stop him."

Bo shook his head, leaned over and was inches from her face, yelling, "Not a chance. I'm leaving you here."

Bo took his jacket and tightly wrapped it around her shoulder tying the arms together under her armpit. He grabbed RD's other hand and placed it firmly over the wound. "Hold this, and don't let go."

He leapt up and ran to a door that she hoped led outside, turning, and shaking the door handle, but unable to get it to open. She watched in horror as he scooped up the tower, lifted it over his head and slammed it down on the door handle.

She screamed out *No!* but he couldn't hear her. The butler on the other side of the hallway door seemed to be kicking the door. Every few seconds it would budge open another quarter of an inch. Bo watched the door for a second, eyes wide, then slammed the tower down two more times, before the handle completely fell off.

One huge kick and fresh air mixed with soft light flooded the room.

RD's vision was going black at the edges and as hard as she tried, she couldn't seem to push hard enough to stop the bleeding.

Bo slammed the tower to the groundbreaking it into pieces. He scooped up the hard drive and ran to RD yelling over the top of the siren.

"Hold on. You hear me? Do not close your eyes. I can't tell you I'm in love with you if you die."

He lifted her body as if she weighed nothing, and when the cool air touched her face, she smiled.

Everything after that faded to black.

~*~

Bo carried RD down a set of concrete stairs in drizzling rain, across an expansive driveway and across what felt under his feet to be thick grass like a putting green. The sky was grey, and it was almost dark. He couldn't have planned the timing any better. He ran, arms aching and legs screaming toward the small patch of woods. If nothing else, he had a gun stowed in the pack he left there. At least he could defend them.

RD moaned, eyes closed.

He was out of breath, but he couldn't let her sleep.

"Woman," he said through gritted teeth, "grip that wound tighter. Don't you dare leave me."

Her good hand pushed his jacket deeper into the wound, and her lids scrunched like she was in pain, but they didn't open.

Bo was only a few feet from the edge of the small woods, when he heard a gunshot from the edge of the house. He crouched down and froze with RD still in his arms, hoping he'd be camouflaged next to the patch of trees. His legs trembled. The butler stood on the landing outside the broken door, shielding his face from the rain and scanned the lake. He'd shot out into the darkness. The angry man stood for a few more seconds scanning. For a brief second he stared toward the woods, seemingly right at them, but in the end, he ran back inside.

Now was his chance.

Bo took a breath and scooped RD tighter into his arms. Taking two large steps he disappeared into the woods. He knew

196

they weren't out of danger yet. Several yards inside the patch of trees his gaze swept the ground. He'd left his backpack at the base of a large oak.

But when he spotted the tree, his pack was gone.

Bo gently set RD against the tree and stood.

Without warning, someone slammed into the side of him knocking him to the ground. Even in the dark, he knew the shape and size of this person. This was someone he'd wrestled with his entire life. His cousin Al.

Only this time, the fight was playful. It was intense and real. This man was so jealous of him and his accomplishments, everything in Bo's mind told him Al would love the chance to choke the life out of him in these dingy woods.

Al sat heavily on his chest making it hard to breathe then rose and swung, hitting him across the cheekbone. The sting of that blow took what breath he had left away. Using an old wrestling move and quick thinking, Bo arched his back and swung a leg around just in time to catch Al off guard. Wrapping both legs around Al's throat Bo slammed him to the ground.

As if they were thirteen again, and after Al was starting to turn purple, he tapped Bo to say let go.

Bo squeezed tighter. The man obviously wanted him dead. This wasn't family. This was jealousy. Jealousy that needed to die.

Al's face turned white. His fingers pulling and tugging at Bo's thighs when he realized his cousin wasn't letting go. In that instant, Bo could see himself as a killer. His cousin had hated him for so long, but more so when his father had died, and Bo became the head of the company instead of Al.

Al made a gurgling noise and slammed his fists into Bo's thigh even harder.

Bo had never wanted to be head of the company. Especially when he'd dug into the nuts and bolts and found out exactly what his uncle and cousin had been exporting.

He realized he wanted the business to die, not necessarily his cousin.

His father's voice behind him, shouted out in English, "Let go!"

Bo did as his father commanded and scrambled to his feet.

This wasn't just another case of the two boys squabbling. This was a fight to the death, despite what his father might have thought.

What Bo didn't notice until after he stood, was his own gun, taken from his backpack, sticking out of his father's hand, pointed at Al.

Al choked and sobbed, speaking in fast Mandarin that his father would've found it shameful the way Bo's father had treated him, shutting down his father's business and taking away his legacy. He yelled that *he* was rightfully the owner. The final decision to continue the business or to shut it down should have been his.

Bo's father looked as though he could spit nails.

He began, "My brother was a shameful man that I loved. Our parents would have disowned him had they known what type of business he ran. I will not condone his legacy of shame, and neither will you."

When Al's breathing had calmed, Bo saw the crazed look in his eyes. It was the same wild look he'd gotten the day he dared Bo to jump off the Henley Street bridge. Bo had refused and Al had called him a coward. He'd tried to force Bo to jump anyway by dragging him toward the side. The only reason he didn't succeed was thanks to a police officer driving by. It was part of the reason Bo had wanted to become a lawyer. To uphold the law.

Al smiled, then took two quick steps toward Bo's father and tried to grab the gun. The two men struggled as Bo ran toward them. When the gun went off, Bo's cousin dropped to the ground.

Bo's father stared at his nephew for a beat, grabbed up Bo's backpack and began trotting toward the road.

Bo scooped up RD, her eyes wide open having heard the gun at such close range. His jacket was soaked with blood.

"Father!" Bo yelled as the rain started pounding heavier.

Bo's father turned back.

"Where are you going?"

"The car. We have to get her to a hospital or she's going to die."

"Father. What about Al?"

"Leave him," his father said, still walking.

"If we take her to a hospital, they will ask questions."

He turned, red faced and angry, "So you want to let her die?"

Bo looked down at RD. No. No, he most definitely did not want that.

His father spun and ran toward his car which was hidden next to several bushes. Carefully, they loaded RD in the car.

When his father sped off, he prayed they'd get her help in time.

Chapter Thirty-Eight

Norris, TN

The limo bounced down the bumpy lake road like an old horse drawn wagon. When it pulled onto the smooth driveway, only the windshield wipers fighting the rain were brave enough to make any noise.

As if he'd rather have been anywhere but there, the driver got out, slammed the door, and walked inside the garage.

D'Angelo looked at his phone then calmly placed it back in his jacket pocket.

Too calmly.

Gianna couldn't take the silence anymore.

"What happened? Do you want to talk about it?"

He smiled, ingenuine and not touching his eyes. He scooted toward her, sitting on the edge of the leather seat, watching her.

Finally, he spoke, "Leo...has been murdered."

He waited, letting his sentence set in, then continued.

"By your daughter."

Gianna didn't have enough acting chops in her entire body to not be taken down by that sentence.

She gasped, "No!"

D'Angelo nodded, "And my father, who was there trying to help me, also died."

Gianna's mind started spinning. Kirin's text indicated they'd all made it out alive. Good girl. But now, she'd have to deal with the fallout of this volatile man losing his father and his oldest childhood frenemy, all at the same time.

She feared that no amount of charm was going to save her now.

"I'm...I'm sorry," was all she could muster.

The driver walked out of the open garage door carrying what looked like a large, black garbage bag. He disappeared around the back of the home, but when he returned, he carried two things: a large umbrella and a wad of bright blue flowers.

As if a light switch had been flicked on, D'Angelo quickly shed his tux jacket, grabbed Gianna by the arm and pushed open the limousine door, shoving her out the door ahead of him, but not letting go of the tight grip he had on her arm.

"Ow!" she said as strongly as her terrified voice could muster. The strap on her heel broke as she was thrust out of the car. He slammed the door, yanking her body next to him as he set out toward the lake.

"Unhand me!" she yelled, then added, "Where are we going?" All the while she pulled and tugged at his immovable fingers that were making bruises on her arm.

As they rounded the corner of the house, the driver, looking as terrorized as she was sure she did, followed them with the umbrella over both their heads. D'Angelo's strides were longer than Gianna's especially since she only had one shoe. She stumbled once and he'd side-eye glared at her as if she'd done it on purpose.

When they reached the top of the stone steps leading down toward the dock, she knew now why he'd asked her if she could swim.

She'd lied and he knew it.

She'd always hated swimming from a very young age. Drowning was by far her biggest fear.

Gianna threw her body down into a sitting position, which caused his body to pitch sideways, slide in the mud and almost fall over the top of her. She'd caught him off guard.

Quickly she yanked off the only heel that was left and used the sharp edge to whack him in the fingers that were still holding her.

D'Angelo yelped and instinctively let go. Gianna scrambled up, lifting the gown above her knees and began to run for her life.

202

She knew that if she got near that lake, she was dead.

Gianna made it about four steps when she was tackled and crushed from behind.

D'Angelo turned her over, completely covered in mud and punched her in the face. Searing pain spread like fire through her cheeks and eyeballs. She screamed out in pain.

With a yell of frustration, D'Angelo grabbed both her arms and began to drag her body toward the steps. He yelled at the driver, who watched in horror, to get something from the garage. When the driver glanced from D'Angelo to Gianna and back, he quickly moved.

Gianna fought with everything she had. She screamed, kicked, and flailed her body in the mud. She tried wrapping her slippery legs around the poles that held up the handrail. Nothing worked.

He slid her body down the sharp steps. Each hard rock step would knock the wind out of her, making it harder and harder to fight back.

When he got her to the bottom, she swung her legs around and tried to take his knees out. He anticipated it, caught it, dropping her hands and drug her by her feet down the long dock toward the boathouse.

The gown she'd worn was now choking her and gathering around her face and ears. She dug her fingers into anything they passed. At one point, she'd reached out and grabbed a wayward deck chair, hoping it would get stuck, make too much noise or at least buy her some time.

Halfway down the dock, D'Angelo stopped and dropped her legs. She pushed her dress down and sat up. Her back was scratched up and bleeding, she tasted blood in her mouth, one of her eyes was almost completely swollen shut. When he stomped toward her, she recoiled, holding one hand up to shield her face. Clearly out of breath, D'Angelo bent close enough to talk to her but not close enough that she could reach him.

"Why are you doing this?" She cried.

D'Angelo said nothing, he only smiled at her, then nodded to someone behind her.

As she turned, she felt the cloth cover her mouth and nose. Then nothing.

Chapter Thirty-Nine

Norris, TN

When Gianna finally came to, her dress had been straightened, her hands and feet tied neatly, and she'd been gagged. She lay at the end of the dock, inside a long black body bag with something cold and scratchy at the bottom. Her toes wiggled slightly. Rough and cold. Her stomach quivered. It was a cinder block.

D'Angelo was several feet away untangling and cutting some rope. The driver was nowhere to be found.

A strange sickly-sweet smell invaded her senses. She looked down at her hands. Tucked gently inside her fingers were blue flowers. The same ones she'd seen the driver holding.

He must've placed them here before they got out of the car. Wait. She recognized those flowers. They were from the bush in the front flower bed.

Gianna's body started to quake.

That's when her movement must've caught his eye.

D'Angelo turned slowly, with an unmistakably evil smile.

He stalked toward her, slowly, like a cheetah evaluating his prey and yet giddy as if he could erase all the bad things that had happened with this one death.

When he was about a foot from her, he crouched down, and spoke.

"I'm sorry it didn't work out between us. I had stellar hopes that a woman of your caliber could learn to live with a man like me. As it stands, both you and your daughter will need to die to make retribution for the two people I lost."

Gianna tried to speak through the gag but couldn't. He shot her a warning look that said, *don't try anything*, then he moved the gag away from her mouth and onto her throat.

"You've killed this way before," she said it as unfeeling and cold as she could muster. Trying desperately to keep the fear out of her voice.

D'Angelo cocked his head to one side and answered, "Of course."

"How many?" she asked.

D'Angelo thought for a second as he secured the rope to the top of the bag.

"Counting you—six. A half dozen."

"I'm going to demand the death penalty."

"Let me know how that works out for you. Your daughter will be in Hell right behind you."

It was then she came unglued. Gianna started thrashing her body, screaming, and cursing. When she lifted her legs, he shoved them back down and began zipping her up. When he got past her chest, he quickly shoved the rag back up covering her mouth.

If his fingers had come just a half inch closer, she could've bitten him and maybe bought some more time.

She was gonna die.

God, she'd been a bad human. She'd planned to spend the rest of her days making up for all the bad she'd done. Hell, it's why she became a lawyer. But now, she'd never see her daughter Paloma again, nor meet Arianna. The girls would always be hunted by this man.

And she'd never get to tell Steve that he was her only true love. Why hadn't she told him when she had the chance? Fear. Fear and feeling unworthy. And now she was going to die in the most heinous ways without him knowing.

That hurt worse than anything.

Gianna started to cry.

D'Angelo took one look at her with zero emotion or regret and began zipping the bag past her neck toward the top of her head.

The zipper made it to her lips when out of nowhere, something hard hit D'Angelo's body knocking him over.

A thick branch as big as her leg fell onto the deck between D'Angelo and her.

For a moment, she thought it might have been a sign from God. Maybe she wasn't doomed after all. A shadow of a man hidden by a ski mask and dressed all in black, stepped over the top of her. Quick as a cat, he grabbed D'Angelo by the neck lifting him off the ground.

D'Angelo screamed, gasped, and kicked holding up his weight by pulling at the man's forearms.

Gianna kicked herself into survival mode. She'd have to use every trick she could if she was gonna get out of this bag. Utilizing her tongue she worked the gag out of her mouth, resting it on her chin. Then she bit the zipper and drug it down a few inches. Shoving off the cinder block at the bottom of the bag with her toes, she wiggled her body as far up as she could while her hands tried desperately to get one another out of the rope binding them. Turning her shoulders, she spun her body onto her stomach and then inched out the opening of the bag using her knees.

Gianna's body was about a foot out of the bag when D'Angelo swung his knees, hitting the man in just the wrong spot. Instantly the man released his tight grip and both men fell on the dock.

The larger man, clearly in pain, stood first, arms up, prepared for a fist fight, but D'Angelo had other plans.

He rose with a large, serrated knife he'd used to cut the rope. He smiled at the man, who smiled back as if to say, bring it.

D'Angelo dove for the man. As they wrestled on the deck, the man in black got in a few punches to D'Angelo's face, stunning him, but D'Angelo had obviously fought with knives before. Both men stood. D'Angelo juked and dove getting his opponent in just the right stance, until he spun around him and sliced him in the belly.

It was then, she heard the man yelp, and she froze. She knew that voice.

Within seconds and with a renewed sense of urgency, Gianna realized her movements weren't nearly fast enough. If she was going to help him, she needed her hands. She tugged and pulled, once even crying out as her skin ripped on her left wrist.

Finally, the rope budged enough she could get one hand out, and then the other.

Quickly she flipped to her side, hugged her knees, and pulled the rope off her ankles.

D'Angelo laughed as the man had one hand up to fight and the other holding the gash on his midsection. Even in the moonlight, she could tell his hand was wet with blood that seeped through his fingers.

The man walked backward toward the end of the dock as D'Angelo walked menacingly toward him with the knife.

"You're gonna die for butting in where you don't belong."

As if he'd just remembered her, D'Angelo turned slightly with his knife still trained on the man and looked for Gianna. The bag was still there, but he couldn't see her.

"Woman! I will find you and when I do, your whole family will die!"

Without warning, the man laid an uppercut to D'Angelo's chin with a force that should have knocked him out. When he landed flat on his back, it took him a second to move.

The man landed on top of D'Angelo, pinning the hand with the knife. They rolled several times until they were once again at the edge of the dock. D'Angelo got his knife hand free and scrambled around the injured man, knocked him off balance and pinned him at the edge of the dock with his head hanging over. His good hand that wasn't holding his wound was trapped by D'Angelo's foot, while his knee and the rest of his weight was sitting squarely on the man's chest.

D'Angelo lifted the knife with both hands high above his head, poised and ready to kill him.

Gianna screamed out. She swung the heavy tree branch with every ounce of strength she had left, hitting him squarely in the head.

The knife flew into the water at almost the same time as D'Angelo's body.

Gianna ran to the man lying at the end of the dock. She pulled off his ski mask and used it to apply pressure to the gash on his abdomen.

"Hi honey," Steve said weakly.

"Don't talk, okay."

It was then floodlights and yelling began, ordering them to stand with their hands up. Gianna placed Steve's hand over his wound and did as they commanded.

She quickly explained Steve's position and the reason he couldn't comply. She also explained that the real evil was currently drowning at the bottom of the lake.

The FBI, who'd been tipped off anonymously, called an ambulance for Steve and Gianna, secured the house and everyone in it and would spend the next two days dredging around the doc and the rest of the cove.

She knew they'd find D'Angelo and five more women.

Gianna wasn't the sixth, he was.

As paramedics loaded Steve into the ambulance, he refused to let go of Gianna. And for her part, she refused to let go of him.

Once they were loaded, paramedics set up an IV and began working on his wound. The weight of it all came crashing down. Gianna sobbed into her hands.

"G. G look at me." Steve batted the paramedics away and reached for her.

Gianna wiped her eyes, then scooted forward onto the bench and gave him a hand.

"You're safe. I got you."

"I almost…lost my chance." Her voice shook.

"For what?" he asked, pulling her closer.

Gianna stood and lowered her face to his so that their foreheads touched. She closed her eyes and answered.

"To ask you to marry me."

Chapter Forty

Corryton, TN

Two weeks later

Kirin stared at her reflection.

Cream colored silk hugged her body, of course, extra tight around her midsection. Her nails had been painted a calming pale pink that matched her lips. Frederick had de-Frankenstein'd her and set her color back to her original yellow blonde, then swept it up and gracefully pinned it into a gorgeous knot with a few soft, strands framing her face.

Alone for the first time all afternoon, she closed her eyes briefly and enjoyed the silence, knowing it wouldn't last. Long shadows, even through drawn curtains, told her it was almost time.

They'd purposefully blocked her view of the soft grass just in front of the woods. The place where in about an hour, she'd marry the man of her dreams.

A soft double knock rang out toward the bottom of her bedroom door and then it cracked open a hair.

"Mama?" Little Jack's lips touched the opening.

Kirin turned and straightened her dress.

"Okay, I'm ready."

Her two young men walked in dressed in light grey suits, starched white shirts, and baby pink ties. Jack ran toward her, "Mama, you look pretty!" he said and hugged her.

Will stood like a statue next to the door, his mouth hung open. He was almost her height now, minus her heels. She held both hands out and he came toward her, embracing her. "Wow, mom. Just wow."

She knew soon enough he'd go through the rebellious teenage years, so she tried to savor every hug.

Something crashed right outside the door and then a quick, "Sorry."

Will shook his head smiling.

"You ready?"

"You sure it's tight?"

Will nodded and grinned, "Might be the reason he's knocking into things."

Little Jack ran back to the door and opened it slowly. "Sam, you sure you can't see? How many fingers am I holding up?" Little Jack held up three.

"Eleven—*oof*," Sam answered, arms out like a mummy and whacking his shoulder on the door frame. Will strutted toward him and grabbed him by the arm, leading him toward Kirin.

"Wait, what are you *wearing*?" Kirin's nose wrinkled up like she'd smelled black licorice.

Sam smiled, head tilted up, proud of his attire. "My faded navy sweats with grease stains and the holey t-shirt I wear to work on the cars. Didn't want you seeing *me* before the wedding. It'd be bad luck."

Will shook his head like it was the dumbest thing in the world and Kirin smiled. Sam reached out for her, and she took his hand.

"Boys, give us just a second, okay?"

Will started toward the door, but little Jack stood in front of Sam and waved, making extra sure he couldn't see. He was taking his role of being on the "best man" team very seriously.

Kirin laughed.

Sam's face quickly went somber.

"Feeling okay?" he asked, reaching up to touch her face.

She leaned into his hand and closed her eyes. "Yeah. Just nervous. The idea of walking down that aisle and everyone staring at me..."

"You'll have the boys."

"I know. It's still intimidating, though."

Sam gently stroked her cheek, "I'm glad you finally told me what happened when I was gone." Eyes still covered, he hung his head and shook it. "Let's not do that again, okay?"

212

Kirin gently wrapped her hands around his face, pulling it inches from hers, "Sam Neal. If you'll get out of these dreadful clothes, and meet me down front, near the priest, I'll be yours forever."

Her friend Stacy swept into the room, in her pale pink bridesmaid dress, and with perfect timing said, "You heard her. Go get naked and we will see you at the wedding. Now shoo!"

Sam laughed as Stacy grabbed him by the shoulders and led him out of the room. Once he was clear of the doorway, she wheeled Laura inside and parked her next to the bride, then closed the door behind them.

Laura, dressed in a pink gown herself, sat in her wheelchair fluffing Kirin's flowers, and trying her best not to scowl. Understandably, she was upset because although she was finally starting to walk, she wasn't adept enough yet to do anything but roll down the aisle for her friend. Kirin glanced over and immediately Laura grinned.

Stacy flitted around tugging and straightening the hem of Kirin's train, until it was a perfect circle. That was until Kirin would laugh or use her arms to tell a story, and mess it up. Stacy would jokingly complain and start all over.

Three knocks at the door sent Stacy into a tizzy.

"Sam Neal, if that's you again, I swear, I'm gonna beat your ass!"

"It's not," came the formal female voice on the other side of the door.

Stacy and Laura looked at each other eyebrows up, then to Kirin, who smiled widely, nodding to let her in.

Stacy opened the door.

Gianna always looked radiant, but today she damn glowed. For once, Kirin didn't feel that pull of jealousy or hatred, only love.

Gianna smiled politely at Laura and Stacy—still hesitant and guarded. When they returned it, her lips briefly changed to a grim line, until she saw Kirin.

Kirin held out both hands and Gianna's face lit up.

"G, you look amazing!" Kirin said, pulling her friend in for a squeeze.

Since their ordeal, Kirin was slowly getting Gianna used to hugging, but today, Gianna squeezed back, clearly grateful to have her friendship.

When they pulled back, Gianna held Kirin at arm's length and let out a very masculine whistle. "Stunning. Part of me thought you'd have on the homely scrubs." They both laughed, then Gianna turned serious. "My childhood friend is going to cry when he sees you."

Kirin nodded, "I hope so."

Gianna pointed at Kirin's belly, "Little G is looking cute today."

Kirin touched her small belly and laughed, "I like the name *Katherine* myself."

Gianna laughed and counted on her fingers, "I'm voting for, number one—healthy and number two— totally in love with her Aunt Gianna who, by the way, plans to spoil the stuffing out of her."

"And what if *she* happens to be *he*?"

"Well, I'll spoil the crap out of him, too." Gianna said waving her arms.

Kirin froze.

She lifted Gianna's left hand.

It sparkled.

"About time," Kirin said, pinning G with her eyes.

Gianna looked down at the ring and shrugged, still wearing her mask of feigned disinterest, "I know. He asks me every day when I'm gonna wear it. I guess today is as good as any, right?"

Stacy stepped forward and laid a hand gently on Gianna's arm. "You've made my brother so happy. Thank you."

Gianna genuinely returned her smile, then added, "I hope he knows what he's doing. It's not gonna be easy, living with somebody like me and the girls."

Stacy smiled at her, then went back to pulling at Kirin's train.

"Is it getting any better?" Kirin whispered to Gianna who in response rolled her eyes.

"Paloma seems much happier now that her sister is home with us. She's still her loving, optimistic, self.

214

Arianna…" Gianna trailed off then began again, "Suffice it to say she's *exactly* like I was at that age. Takes a mighty big storm to knock down all the walls she's put up."

Kirin giggled. She couldn't help it.

Gianna glared playfully, "Laugh it up, but there's a reason some animals eat their young." She sighed heavily, "Oh, but on a good note, Arianna *adores* Steve. Thinks he's the greatest thing since sliced cheese." Sarcasm dripped from her voice as she waved her hands theatrically. "Me however…well it might take *years* to make Ari like me."

Kirin waited until their eyes met, then grinned at her friend, "It took me years to like you, but I did it. She will too. You'll see."

Gianna smiled gratefully.

Three more knocks at the door made Stacy curse under her breath and run to open it. She cracked it, whispered something then ushered someone inside.

When Kirin turned, Rosa stood frozen with her mouth open.

When the older woman's eyes began to mist, Kirin wagged a finger at her, "Uh-uh. Don't do that. You promised."

Rosa wiped her eyes, raised her chin, set her jaw, and said, "Your parent's picture is on its stand, your aunt Kathy and uncle Dean have just been seated, and your uncle wanted me to remind you that if the boys didn't behave and walk you down the aisle properly, he'd gladly carry both of them by their ears and do the job for them. Oh, and Arthur refused to sit on your side since Sam doesn't have much family. He grumbled something about owing it to Jack.

And finally, your groom skipped down the aisle like a five-year-old. Now he's standing next to the priest, wringing his hands. Will keeps looking at his watch and Little Jack is doing cartwheels in the back—too close to the food table I might add, to entertain the crowd until you get there."

Kirin shook her head and smiled. It wouldn't have been her wedding if it wasn't a three-ring circus.

~*~

RD waited patiently as Bo ran around the car. He smiled brightly like she was the most beautiful woman in the world as he opened the door and helped her out of the car. When the strap on her gown fell, with soft, caring fingers he resituated it over the white bandage on her shoulder.

He'd had way too much fun earlier helping her get dressed.

Twice.

Holding Bo's hand, RD spotted her aunt across the sea of chairs toward the front. The woman's gaze was wild and frazzled as if she were running the show and it was falling apart.

When their gazes locked, RD smiled, and her aunt waved and smiled back.

Aunt Rosa hadn't left her side the entire time RD was in the hospital. Even kicking Bo out, a time or two, so he'd go home and take a shower. It didn't matter that she'd explained over and over that nothing was her aunt's fault. She carried it and for that RD felt bad.

Bo's father had taken the fall for all of it, keeping Bo's name completely out of it. At first, he'd been arrested with zero bond, until Gianna stepped in, bailed him out and spoke on his behalf to the judge explaining that he took over his younger brother's business without knowledge of what it entailed.

When Bo led her toward a seat, a large man stood before them blocking the way and eclipsing the setting sun behind him.

Steve nodded and she nodded back.

"Your intel provided everything we needed."

"Thank you, sir." RD answered, stiffening up as she always did around her kind.

"I've put in a request to keep you as an agent in the Intelligence and Criminal Services but added a request to send you to Quantico for a month to learn cyber hacker training."

RD's eyes lit up, "Thank you, sir."

Steve's demeanor immediately relaxed, and he offered her a hand, "On a personal note, RD...I'm grateful to you and very proud of you."

It was the first time someone on her team hadn't called her *Rookie*.

RD smiled and took Steve's outstretched hand.

Steve looked up and his eyes brightened. He excused himself and walked toward the back. RD turned to see the bridesmaids starting to line up to walk down the aisle. Gianna's gaze swept the crowd and when it landed on RD, a knowing smile spread across her face. She tilted her head toward RD, who returned the gesture.

When Bo led her to their aisle seats and sat, he immediately dropped her hand and stared straight ahead.

RD watched him for a beat, then whispered as the music started, "for the record," Bo turned and watched her, cautiously, "You never told me. You said you were gonna tell me, but technically you never did."

Bo leaned forward, resting his elbows on his knees, and clasping his hands tightly. He turned his gaze toward her.

"After all we've been through, you think I don't?"

RD shook her head and said, "No, I think, after all we've been through, I can't say it until you do. And I *want* to say it."

Bo shook his head and grinned, then turned his body toward hers, taking both of her hands in his.

"Are you always gonna make everything this difficult?'

"Yep," she answered without hesitation.

Bo pinned her with his eyes. "Rosita, I am in love with you."

RD's gaze went blurry, but she said it before she could overthink it.

"And I love you, Bo."

Careful not to hurt her, Bo pulled her in gently.

She knew he'd never let her go.

~*~

Arthur had dressed up the split rail fence that divided their property from his in strips of white garland. White twinkling lights crisscrossed back and forth overhead, while the sun sunk down behind trees, not yet retired, but close enough to cause the cicadas to hum.

Soft harp music played to guests filling black chairs that lined both sides of a long white carpet. In front, standing under an overfilled arch spilling with pink and white flowers, stood her Sam.

Kirin stood behind the crowd, she could see him, but he hadn't yet spotted her.

The man who'd saved her, both physically and mentally. The man who'd believed in her and chose her when he could've chosen his old life. The same man who adored her father and promised he'd take care of her.

Kirin's eyes misted over.

Squeezing her right hand, Will waited until she glanced at him then mouthed, "Love you, mom." Kirin mouthed back, "Love you too, boy."

Little Jack bounced happily on her left until Rosa turned, smiled sweetly at her then gave him the stink eye. He nodded understanding and when Kirin looked down at him, he glanced up and winked at her.

Gianna strode down the aisle first. She stopped briefly when she got to Rosa's niece and held out a hand. The two briefly grabbed hands and exchanged smiles and then she continued.

Steve's body language standing up with Sam changed immediately from FBI tough and stiff to smiling like a kid when he saw his girl crush.

From Kirin's vantage point, she couldn't tell, but Gianna must've stuck her tongue out or flipped Sam off as she passed him. He rolled his eyes and shook his head.

Next was Laura. Since her job was to hold Kirin's flowers and her own, they'd made special holders on the back of her wheelchair for both bouquets. Her husband Adam, dressed better than she'd ever seen him, pushed her chair down the aisle right to where she should stand.

Lastly was Stacy, thinner than normal, but smiling and happy. Brandon sat at Sam's side and blew her a kiss as she quickly got into place.

When the music changed to *Canon in D*, Kirin squeezed both boys' hands. They'd practiced walking slow, turning the corner and pausing, then walking down the aisle.

But when they turned the corner and paused, Kirin froze.

Sam wasn't there.

He wasn't waiting for her at the front like he'd promised.

218

She stared at the spot where he'd just been. Then glanced around. Her feet wouldn't move.

Will and Little Jack let go of her hands and it broke her trance. Smiling, both boys walked down the aisle ahead.

Strong, warm fingers interlaced hers. When she looked up, there stood Sam, right next to her with tears in his eyes.

"You look breathtaking."

Sam wiped a tear that escaped with his other hand then continued, "I protected you for far too long to let you feel alone or fearful on the best day of my life."

Kirin let out the breath she hadn't realized she was holding, leaned into him, and smiled.

Little Jack ran back down the aisle carrying her huge bouquet of flowers. He handed them to his mama, winked and ran back up the aisle.

Slowly, they walked toward the front, hand in hand.

Together at last.

The end.

Turn the page to read an excerpt from Kelley's newest Series starting Fall of 2023

Mary Catherine Hall
Cozy Mystery Series
A-Z

A Murder in the Closet

Book One

By
Kelley Griffin

Chapter One

Death followed her.

No *really*, it did.

When Mary Catherine Hall or 'Cat' as she was known to her fellow private school teachers, had moved from her empty existence in Coldwater, Michigan to the postcard small town of Fountain City, Tennessee, almost a year ago, she'd longed to escape her lifelong reputation and outrun her notoriety.

And she'd accomplished it.

Well almost.

It wasn't like she killed people. Heavens no. Death was never *her* fault. That would be illogical. She couldn't even squash a mosquito if it were sucking all the blood out of her. She'd feel too sad for ending its life. Yeah. Catholic guilt was alive and prevalent in her life, for sure.

Cat had made it through almost an entire school year—all but the last two weeks—without that heavy shadow.

In her first-year teaching at St. Frances de Sales Elementary, she'd gained the respect and admiration of the administration and the other teachers and even with her quirky ways and unconventional teaching style, her 2nd graders' scores were through the roof. She'd even been one of the youngest teachers in the diocese nominated for teacher of the year.

And yet somehow, she always managed to land smack dab in the middle of a homicide.

Most days she wished for normal.

Like today.

As she stood over the contorted body of Nelson Hawkins, the school janitor, inside the janitorial closet, she knew today wasn't going to end well.

This was a bad sign.

She believed in signs just like she believed saying a rosary warded off all things evil. Under her breath, she swore this month's made-up curse word, *flarkstack.*

Cat was seasoned enough not to touch anything but found herself logging the scene in her mind. Nelson's normally kind, albeit wrinkled face was scrunched into a scowl. Nelson was a harmless, quiet flirt. He loved elbowing the kids and staff alike and always had a goofy joke to tell them. Beloved. That's what he was. His hearing aid lay flopped out of his ear next to his head and his deep-set brown eyes peered up toward the ceiling as if he were looking at the stars.

On closer observation, however, his skin was littered with tiny dots as if he'd been sprayed in the face with a plant mister. The room was disheveled as if there'd been a struggle. And a spray can of cleaning fluid had been propped up next to his hand on the floor. Long bony fingers splayed straight out —not wrapped around the can, but the can touched them. The mops and brooms lay scattered as if someone took an open bag of pretzel sticks and threw them in the air.

Cat shut the door behind her and pulled out her radio.

"Mrs. Hatmaker?"

"Yes?"

"Switch to channel 9."

After a breath Cat spoke into the radio again, "Can you ask Principal Zimmer to come to the janitorial closet, please."

"I'll find him and send him right there."

Mrs. Hatmaker worked in the school for thirty years. She was almost as wide as she was tall, wore her hair in the exact same high clip every day with her reading glasses propped on the top of her head. She prided herself in knowing every inch of that school plus every soul that had inhabited it during her tenure. But lately, her memory had started to falter, and she was more than ready for her retirement in two weeks. She told everyone who'd listen. They'd already held her retirement party after school one evening last week in the library.

Mr. Andy Zimmer was a relatively young Principal at only thirty-four. He was five years older than Cat and in the short time she'd known him, he'd proven himself to be wise and kind. He was fair and believed in his teachers, treating them like rare commodities. He'd had faith in her and in one short year, he'd been one of the best bosses she'd ever had. The best part was that the kids from Pre-k to eighth grade respected him and wanted to rise to his high expectations.

A year ago, he'd been thrilled to help hire Cat to take over for their retiring 2nd grade teacher. He'd interviewed her only once, having already had a conversation with her old principal about her faith and her skills as a teacher. And when she'd met him, he'd hired her on the spot.

Her face warmed. She wondered what he'd think of her now. There hadn't been a single case where she wasn't a suspect at least once.

When she landed the job, she'd flown home, packed her things, grabbed her cat *Skittles* and flown back the very next day.

She hadn't even looked back. There was nothing for her there anyway. All that was left in her hometown were gravestones.

When Mr. Zimmer opened the door, he shut it quickly behind him. His smile diminished quickly into a grim line, and he gasped. It took him a full ten seconds to get his bearings and take in his surroundings.

"Oh, God," Mr. Zimmer whispered then clamped his hand over his mouth. When he found his voice, he asked, "Heart attack?"

Cat glanced from Nelson's body back up to Mr. Zimmer, "My gut says no."

Mr. Zimmer looked at Cat like he was seeing her for the first time.

"No?"

"Look at his neck."

Mr. Zimmer leaned over the body. When he reached out to steady himself by holding on to a grey metal shelf to get a closer look, Cat grabbed his hand and shook her head. He immediately put his hands behind his back and squinted toward Nelson's neck.

A slender, plastic, nearly invisible line wrapped around his pale skin twice. Already it'd caused a purple line to appear as if someone had traced it with a felt tip marker. Mr. Zimmer whipped out his cell and called the superintendent, the authorities and Mrs. Hatmaker on a secure line. At Cat's request, he asked if someone could pick up her second-grade class from P.E. and deliver it to the lunch room.

Within minutes, the authorities arrived and blocked off that part of the hallway. Teachers were notified of a soft lockdown and to take an alternate route. A pop-up privacy screen was brought in so the investigators could open the door of the tiny closet and take pictures.

Cat stood off to the side and waited for the questions she knew would come.

~*~

Detective Joseph 'Rand' Fulton couldn't believe his luck.

Fridays were supposed to be relatively calm now that he'd been promoted to dayshift. But of course, he got called to a midday homicide. And to beat it all, he had to walk back in to visit his old elementary school. A place he loathed with a passion.

He wondered if mean old Sister Bernadette was there. God, that nun hated him. Then again, she was old as Methuselah when he was there, and he'd been a punk. No way she was still teaching. Or breathing.

As Rand and his newbie partner strutted through the front doors and up the stairs he was taken aback by the smell—lemony clean and the exact same way he remembered from his youth. The tile floor with its brown and cream pattern looked like it hadn't changed a bit. The trophy case just to the left of the office, where they'd placed their perfect season basketball trophies all three years he played, looked like it hadn't been touched since he left. All the memories came flooding back.

How could it still smell the same? Involuntarily, he smiled. Rand glanced up and stared at the same statue of St. Frances de Sales that greeted him every morning of his youth.

Truth be told, he'd had some great memories at that tiny school. Made some lifelong friends, too. Then again, this was where he'd lost his love of God and all things religion.

That, he brushed out of his mind.

226

He was sure this call would be anything but routine. The male principal met him at the top of the stairs, checked their credentials and led them down the elementary hallway.

As he took in the scene, he noticed a petite young teacher standing off to the side. Her brown hair was pulled tight into a bun at the base of her neck. Her white starched button down with a rounded collar was cinched tight. He'd almost mistook her for a student, except he'd spotted her staff lanyard. Not a speck of dirt on her or a hair out of place. She was the epitome of every Catholic School teacher he'd ever had. And, God, she was tiny. She couldn't have been five feet tall.

Since when did teachers wear the same type of uniforms as the kids? That was new since he was there. The petite teacher had porcelain skin that looked like she never went outside, anchored by scorching eyes the color of whiskey that locked onto him the moment she'd spotted him. She looked familiar, but he couldn't place her. He scratched the back of his neck feeling suddenly self-conscious. It nagged at him. He'd seen her somewhere before.

God, he hoped he didn't *know* her from one of his cornhole parties. That would be awkward.

She glanced down toward the floor and shook her head. This puzzled him for half a beat before he took out his phone and began videoing the scene.

The victim was a grey headed thin man, wearing blue jeans and a grey t-shirt with whisps of cotton hair messy on his head. He looked to be approximately seventy years old, lying flat on his back inside a closet. His legs were bent at an unnatural angle. And he had something tied around his neck.

Rand's newbie partner Ken looked as pale and clammy as the victim. He tiptoed around like he was stalking a tiger as he snapped static pictures and logged the scene. *Rookie*. Death was nothing new to Rand. He'd worked the third shift drug and gang scene prior to being promoted to Desk jockey—er Detective.

Rand pulled out gloves and stepped gingerly into the space. The only sound was the shutter on Ken's camera clicking every few seconds. This was no accident. The top two shelves were neat and untouched, but the bottom two had been jostled. Whoever did this took the janitor by surprise. But according to the principal, the school was locked up tight. They'd been buzzed in through an outside gate, then the front door, and they'd had to reveal credentials before they were brought back to the space. All initial clues led to this being an inside job.

Andy Zimmer stepped forward and indicated the young teacher had found the body. She didn't seem as shook up as he'd have expected her to be. Curious. After spending a good bit of time with the body and with team two who'd arrived and were wrapping the janitor and loading him into the ambulance, Rand took off his gloves, took out his notepad and stalked toward her.

When she saw him coming, she stood up tall, which was to say *not tall*, but straightened her back, kicked back her shoulders, and plastered on one of the fakest smiles he'd ever seen.

"Hi, I'm detective—"

"I know who you are," she cut him off.

His head cocked to the side like a dog hearing a silent whistle. "You do?"

"Sure, you're the detective they've assigned to the case, and you are inept at laundry."

Rand shook his head. "I'm sorry? *What?*"

"You leave your laundry in the washer too long, it smells." She walked past him toward the office and motioned for him to follow.

Rand absentmindedly smelled one shoulder. It smelled like it always did. He followed her and when she turned sideways and cracked a smile, he knew he'd been played.

He stopped walking and narrowed his eyes, "Have we met? Ms....?"

The teacher stopped briefly and turned, "*Miss.*"

"Miss?"

"Hall. Catherine Hall. But you may call me Cat when we're not with the students."

"Cat, I'll ask again, have we met?"

Miss Hall ignored his question, turned, and walked into the front office.

Now this place was the land that time forgot. Brown carpet, clean yet worn and there sat old Mrs. Hatmaker. She dabbed at one eye with a handkerchief, then narrowed her eyes and nodded at him as if to say she knew he'd be back in the principal's office one more time.

Cat took a sharp right just past Mrs. Hatmakers counter and headed toward the conference room next to the principal's office. This hallway he unfortunately knew well. He followed. Jesus she could walk fast with those tiny legs.

She answered back over her shoulder, "Yes, but you wouldn't remember it."

As they rounded another corner, she opened a door, flipped on the light, and sat at an oval mahogany table surrounded by eight chairs.

He entered the room with his gaze fixed on her face and watched her as he pulled out a chair and sat.

"Tell me." He demanded.

A cute as hell grin spread across her face and shook her head.

"Shouldn't you be asking about the dead body I found?"

Just then, Mr. Zimmer and Ken rounded the corner into the room followed by an older woman dressed in heels and a skirt. The woman's chubby face was red and blotchy. Then a young priest looking terrified sat along with the school counselor. Suddenly the room seemed too full, and all eyes were on him.

He shot Cat a look saying they weren't finished, cleared his throat then flipped open his notebook, took out his phone and hit record. He stated his full name and then asked everyone in the room to do the same. He nodded to her last.

"Mary Catherine Hall," she stated, chin up and eyes that seemed to see through him.

Of course, with a name like that she'd probably grown up in Catholic schools like him.

"Miss Hall, tell me what you were doing when you found the deceased?"

She answered poised and calm. "At approximately 9:45, I went to find our janitor Nelson, as I had a child leave P.E. walk into my classroom and throw up. The student had just been knocked to the ground playing dodgeball and had a head injury, so I was afraid she had a concussion. I walked her to the clinic, left her with the nurse, then searched for Nelson. I couldn't find him, so I went looking for the janitorial cart. It wasn't inside the teacher workroom like it always is, so I used my classroom key to open the janitorial closet thinking I'd find it there. That's when I found him."

"And did you touch anything inside?"

"No."

"Did you see anyone else in the hallway that you didn't recognize."

Cat didn't miss a beat, "No."

Rand turned to Ken, "You've already secured the visitors log from this morning?"

"Yes, sir. Ten parents stopped in; nine for morning church—er Mass and one dropped off a binder to a fourth grader. All information has been secured on these visitors, but all were long gone by 9am and Nelson was last seen investigating a spot where the roof leaked at the door of the art room around 9:30."

Rand glanced over at Mr. Zimmer. The man stared at the center of the table. His expression was unmistakable.

If nobody except staff were inside the school at the time of the murder, it'd had to be an inside job.

~*~

As news crews arrived and the school was all abuzz with the news of Nelson's death rushing through it like wildfire, Cat tried to console and wrangle her class back together after lunch. The diocese sent counselors to each classroom to help the children and teachers cope with the news. Mr. Zimmer and the superintendent decided to finish out the few hours left in the day that Friday, then close the following Monday, with several counselors set to return with them on Tuesday.

With only a week left in school, this meant Cat needed to fit all her end-of-the-school year plans from five days to four, but she could manage since one of those days was nothing but a party.

The Detective had indicated he had more questions for her but had to interview all that were closest to Nelson as well. And Cat had twenty-three second graders to attend to.

After dismissal, Cat returned to her classroom rubbing the stress from her shoulders. Report Cards were due in four days for the last nine weeks of school and she had several assignments to grade and enter.

As usual, she didn't turn on the fluorescents. With the blinds open, the late afternoon sun lit up the room and not turning on the lights was part of her calm down routine after a long day. She'd only made it a few steps into the room when, focused on the papers on her desk, she froze.

That was the thing about having an eidetic memory. The brain would routinely catalog items, without her even knowing it. She may not have much going for her, but her ability to memorize any room was something she used to be embarrassed about. Now she took pride in it. But just two steps into her room, she knew.

"You moved something on my desk," she announced to the room.

"I didn't mean to," Rand announced, his long body bent as he peered into the fish tank that stood in the corner by the windows. He stared at the unmoving water through the glass littered with bereavement sticky notes written from the students to their latest dead fish.

Cat whipped around and stopped. Their eyes locked. His jaw was clenched tight. Stress lived there. Intense brown eyes pierced hers. Just enough stubble lined his jaw to indicate he hadn't shaved that morning; it dotted his jawline. He stood, towered really, at least a foot over her. Muscles straightened and bulged, especially for someone she never saw out jogging or at the glass fronted gym in the tiny town. He had the kind of face that said he was probably super popular in school and yet his eyes held the possibility of kindness.

Somehow, she'd known he'd be there. Her hands trembled like they did when she was near an attractive man. She needed to switch tactics. Her back straightened.

"Wake up late?"

His eyes narrowed and searched her face, "I did. Do you notice everything?"

"I do." She shot back.

"What did you notice about Nelson today?"

"It was made to look like an accident."

As he pondered her words, he stalked toward her seemingly deliberately slow, touching a desk here and there as he did. She hadn't realized how much he loomed over her until he came close. Too close. He invaded her space. She walked around behind her desk and sat. He pulled up a chair twirled it around and sat backward in it, facing her. "What makes you say that?"

"The can of cleaning fluid," she said, pointedly not looking at him as she began putting stacks of papers to be graded into her backpack, "it was all over his face like he'd sprayed it accidentally on himself."

Rand scratched his chin, "But he didn't?"

"No, if he had, he'd have dropped the can. Most likely, it would've rolled away. It was placed upright, back in front of his outstretched hand, by the killer."

"You don't think it could've landed that way?"

"Not likely. Did you fingerprint it?"

"I can't tell you that."

She froze, looking at him now and shot him a look. At some point he was going to have to trust her. "Okay, but if you did, you wouldn't have found any fingerprints."

Now, he looked perplexed, but his response was patronizing. "Oh really? Why?"

"Because Nelson was very particular about certain areas. He insisted our janitorial room was neat and orderly. The gray rags were meticulously folded. All except one."

Cat saw the twitch in Rand's eye as his jaw tightened. She'd hit a nerve.

Packing again, she continued, "It'd been used and placed back on top by someone who tried to mimic his particular folding style. Someone who *knew* him."

Rand sat, staring at her. Quiet for a beat before speaking, "So, you've done this before?"

"I have," she stated matter-of-factly as she put the last of the papers in her backpack, stood and slung it over her shoulder. She unhooked the carabiner that held her keys and raised an eyebrow at him.

"Are we finished here?"

"For now."

He stood, placing the chair back where he found it. He turned toward her, his gaze pinning her in place. "You realize that I have no suspects...except *one*, right?"

She shrugged. "Wouldn't be the first time. And let's go ahead and get it out of the way that the last thing I said to Nelson yesterday, was in anger."

Rand watched her with a completely frustrating, emotionless look on his face, then followed her out of the classroom into the hallway.

She felt his eyes on her as she locked her classroom door, walked down the hall and out the glass doors toward her car.

Chapter Two

Rand was out of sorts. The tiny woman had gotten under his skin.

He'd been a detective for over two years, how did he miss the rag? Something told him this wasn't her first rodeo. But she had to know that she was the prime suspect. No civilian is that calm around a dead body. Her hands had trembled when she'd discovered him in her classroom. Rand knew full well that wasn't an admission of guilt, but then again, most people don't just randomly shake unless they have something to hide.

And she'd admitted guilt. Rand knew full well people said things in anger all the time, but it didn't make them killers. But still, there was something about her.

Pulling his blacked-out cruiser into his parking spot at the station, he took the concrete steps two at a time, and flung open the glass doors. Through security and down two hallways he came to his CO's office door and knocked.

Captain Jeff Stiles motioned for him to enter but put a finger to his mouth to tell Rand to be silent. He had his grandson, whom he doted on constantly, on speaker and was listening to his day in pre-k. The tiny voice giggled and garbled his speech and Jeff listened intently like his life depended on the conversation. Rand didn't quite understand the granddad bond. Thank God had no kids himself, and he was an only child to aging parents. His grandparents had died way before he was born.

When Jeff hung up, his face immediately fell.

"The principal at St. Joe's. Really? What'd ya find out?"

Rand ran a hand through his hair, "Not much. Transmitted the report about an hour ago."

"I got it," Jeff said, as he typed on his keyboard to pull it up on screen. "What about the teacher who found him, did she see anything?"

"She sees everything," Rand grumbled, more to himself than to his CO. Jeff leaned back and eyed Rand curiously.

"Her name sounded familiar, so I ran a check on her. No record of any felony or misdemeanors, but she seems to have an uncanny knack at helping police find murderers. I talked to the CO near the microscopic town in Michigan where she came from, and they'd used her quite a bit to help them."

Rand shook his head. He didn't see that coming. She seemed so prim and proper. The good Catholic girl had a past of helping the police with murders? No way. Too odd. He just didn't see it.

Jeff leaned forward and pointed a finger at Rand.

"You understand why this case is so important, right?"

Rand nodded but said nothing. His past was never far from his mind.

Jeff continued, "Not that...my grandson is there. Just down the hall from where Nelson was killed. Rand, I want your entire focus on this case. I want you to use whatever is necessary to find out who did this. I don't want my grandson inside a school where murders happen."

Rand nodded and stood.

He knew what he needed to do.

He'd have to use the tiny teacher's help.

Chapter Three

The more you know, the more you know you don't know. ~Aristotle

Ten months.

She'd been in the quaint city ten-flipping-months and death couldn't *wait* to expose her. *Flarkstack.*

This new made-up curse word wasn't cutting the anger she felt pulsing through her veins. Death could've at least let her make a few friends before she became the outcast.

But no.

It reveled in making her stand out in a world she just wanted to fade into. She pulled one long strand of hair out of her eyes and harshly tucked it behind her ear. Feeling sorry for herself was not her norm.

Cat cleaned her apartment like she did every Saturday but this time, with more gusto than usual, then stopped to rest with Skittles for a bit until the feline decided bathing herself took more priority than her owner.

A trip out of the house. Yes, she needed to get out for a bit. She texted her only call-at-any-hour type of friend in the city, and they agreed to meet ten minutes later for ice cream.

For May, East Tennessee had a funny way of showing it was almost summer. Some mornings the weather started out muggy, hot and in the eighties. But other times it'd hovered around fifty-five and left her shivering in her VW.

Today, however it was slated to start out cool, but would reach a mild but sunny seventy-five degrees by noon. Perfect punch-bug weather, especially a convertible. She zipped her jacket patted the top of Bessie, then unhooked the top.

As she pulled out of her apartment complex, a certain detective in his cruiser turned in. She decided to not even look his way. He seemed so oblivious to the world around him, he'd never know the difference.

Of course she'd noticed him, and *he* hadn't noticed her. Story of her life.

Seemed like some people chose to see only what they wanted to see.

Cat turned right and headed for Bruster's. she could almost taste the mint chocolate chip. Ice cream could fix anything, but especially weeks that ended with death. Grading papers and lunch would have to be postponed for creamy delicious ice cream.

As she started up the first hill, Bessie hesitated. Then she sputtered and jerked.

That was odd.

Cat pushed the gas, but she had no power. Nothing. *Perfect.* At the next side street she pulled in and stopped.

She'd noticed the car had been running a little on the hot side, but now smoke poured out from the back.

Cat opened the trunk lid and stepped back. It smelled like a cross between burnt brakes and a plastic milk jug on fire. She stomped back to the driver's side and leaned into the car to retrieve her cell. When she rose back up, she screamed.

A short, thin man stood in front of her, wearing a ballcap pulled down over his eyes and blocking her path back to the rear of her car. Instinctively she backed up. His eyes were downcast, gazing at his shoes.

He looked harmless enough, but so did Jeffrey Dahmer.

Before she could utter a word, he spoke.

"I saw the problem."

"What problem?"

"With your minuscule automobile," he answered, in perfect diction, directly to his shoes.

Cat bent and looked at his face.

Lord.

"Henry, is that you?"

"Yes, ma'am," the shy, odd man answered.

Henry allegedly shared an apartment with his younger brother, a promising attorney who was never home. Cat had met him at the mailboxes, on the stairs and even next to the pool. She'd watched him walk to and from the corner market every morning and every afternoon, which was only about a mile from

238

their apartment complex. His job was to clean-up the parking lot before and after hours.

Cat exhaled and stepped closer. Henry was super intelligent with mild adult Autism, and he was super harmless.

"So what did you see?"

"Your belt flung off into the light green grass," he stated plainly.

Just then, the unmarked car she now knew well pulled up behind her with lights flashing.

Rand jumped out of the car with it still running. His gaze quickly switched from her to Henry and back, eyes narrowed.

"Is this man bothering you?"

She looked at him like he had three heads.

"No. He's helping me."

Rand shot her a look that said she was too trusting. She rolled her eyes. Rand took a few steps closer and spoke to Henry.

"Sir, do you live around here?"

Henry still stared at his shoes, but didn't miss a beat, "The name is Henry. Two apartments down from you, *detective*."

Cat giggled. She wasn't the only person Rand was too busy to see.

Rand's eyes narrowed.

"How do you know where I live?"

Henry answered, "Because you left your clothes in the washer in our building overnight. We all know it is you."

Rand's gaze snapped from Henry's face to Cat's. She shrugged and smiled.

He seemed to ignore the laundry jab and switched quick, as if he'd had a change of heart.

"Thank you, Henry. Now, Miss Hall, what's wrong with your...*car*."

Cat's gaze snapped to his scrunched-up face. He'd looked over Bessie like she was covered in dog poop. His face had contorted when he said the word.

Now this just ticked her off. Nobody picked on Bessie.

"Nothing! She's perfectly fine." Cat announced, louder and angrier than she'd meant to. She patted Bessie's side—of course right on a rusted dent, then quickly crossed her arms and glared at the detective.

When their eyes met, he pressed his lips together and nodded as if to say sorry, then walked back toward the engine to have a look. The car was still running.

"I think your missing…"

"This," Henry said, having already walked over retrieved the belt. He handed it to Cat.

She held it up. A frayed rip, held together only by a few strands of rubber, dangled before her eyes. Useless.

She pulled out her phone and quickly found another one. The only problem was getting there.

As if he read her mind, Rand stepped toward her.

"Come on, I'll take you."

Cat scrunched her face and glanced around as if walking the ten miles to the parts store, might be a better option.

Just then, a much newer red convertible spun around the corner a little too fast and screeched to a halt. The shiny mustang purred compared to her bug which usually sounded more like a sputtering sewing machine.

Smiling a bright white smile like he'd just found gold, was Derrick, her banker. With his car still running, he got out and strutted toward them in his starched white shirt and skinny cut khakis. His style made him look much younger than his actual age.

"Sunshine, you're late for ice cream and you're *never* late," he called out, pulling his shiny designer sunglasses off his face, and grinning like he'd just been introduced on Jimmy Kimmel.

Cat smiled broadly at her friend's impeccable timing.

Rand's eyes narrowed as he watched Derrick. Cat noticed his jaw was once again set, tight.

"Bessie trouble," she announced by way of explanation, walking toward her friend.

Derrick side hugged her, then leaned over toward her engine as if it would bite, laughed at himself, and then stuck out his hand to Rand.

"Derrick," he said lightly.

"Rand," the detective answered, with his brows pulled together as if he were trying to unscramble a word.

Derrick nodded at Henry, who stood a few paces away and threw up a quick wave. Then turned back to Cat. "Sunshine, want me to call a tow?"

"No, but can we run by the parts store before we get ice cream?"

Rand glanced at his watch.

"Sure!" Derrick leaned over to Cat, and commented much louder than needed, "Wanna invite that *yumminess* to go with us?"

With her back to Rand, she shot Derrick a look.

"Your loss. He's handsome and watching you like a hawk, I might add," Derrick whispered the last part as his eyebrows danced.

Cat turned back and locked eyes with Rand.

After a beat Rand spoke. "Miss Hall, I was gonna contact you today. My Chief wants me to interview a few of the parents this afternoon. Mr. Zimmer assured me you'd help with anything that I needed?"

"Sure," she answered trying to sound light, but sounding as if someone just offered her black licorice, which she loathed. "What time?"

"The first interview is at the school around two. Would that work?"

Derrick clapped his hands together, "Oh, a date. Lovely!"

Cat turned back and glared at her friend, to which he bit his lip to stifle a laugh, then nodded to answer Rand's question, waved goodbye to Henry, and climbed into Derrick's sparkly mustang.

As he turned the vehicle around, Cat put her sunglasses on and watched Rand.

The look on his face was a mixture of frustration, curiosity, and something else.

She couldn't put it into words just yet, but it bothered her the rest of the morning.

~End of sample

To preorder go to www.kelleygriffinauthor.com